The Moonclock

The Moonclock

Claudia Von Canon

Houghton Mifflin   Company   Boston   1979

Library of Congress Cataloging in Publication Data

Von Canon, Claudia
    The moonclock.

    SUMMARY: The correspondence to and from a
Viennese couple during 1683 chronicles domestic and
political affairs including the Turks' siege of their city.
    [I.   Vienna – siege, 1683 – Juvenile fiction.]   1.   Vienna –
siege, 1683 – Fiction.   II.   Austria – [History – Leopold I,
1657-1705 – fiction.]
I.   Title
PZ7.V889MO   [Fic]   79-1076

ISBN 0-395-27810-4

ILLUSTRATIONS ON PAGES 19, 67, 102, 112, AND 137 ARE INCLUDED COURTESY OF THE BILD-
ARCHIV DER OSTERREICHISCHEN NATIONALBIBLIOTHEK.

For Michael and Susanna

TO THE FAVORABLE READER:

This is an account of the last year in the life of young Barbara Schretter, wife of Jacob Schretter von Schrettenberg, town councilor of the City of Vienna. She was married to him in 1682 at Christmas and died in childbirth on December 30, 1683.

The story is of my invention. For its background, however, I have drawn exclusively on contemporary sources, such as chronicles, city ordinances, medicine books, household almanacs, political correspondence, testaments, deeds, and court orders.

The characters owe little to my imagination. They all have crossed my path at some time, although under different names and in different garb. I merely assigned them their places in the plot.

The year 1683 saw the Turkish Siege, a turning point in the destiny of Europe.

In 1453 the Turks had taken Constantinople. But after the initial shock of seeing the infidels masters of the Holy Byzantium and, thus, with a foothold on the European continent, the powers of Christendom returned to their own affairs and quarrels. Some of them even enlisted the Sultan's help against assorted enemies.

Meanwhile, the Turks pressed on westward. During the next two hundred years both the Balkans and Hungary fell under Turkish rule. And in the spring of 1683, Caprara, the imperial ambassador in Constantinople, with dismay saw a huge Turkish army setting forth for Vienna, the capital of the Holy Roman Empire.

In this eleventh hour Europe realized that if Vienna fell, the Turks would stable their horses not only in St. Stephen's Cathedral, but sooner or later in St. Peter's in Rome as well. Although help was slow to come, the city, encircled by the enemy and cut off from the Imperial Army, held out. It was Vienna's finest hour. In this book I am happy to allow my hometown to put its best foot forward.

Writing this book was an enjoyable task, made even more enjoyable through the generous help of friends:

Richard M. Douglas, professor of history, M.I.T.

Linda I. Solow, music librarian, M.I.T.

Barry Spacks, who contributed the graceful translation of *Begli Occhi*.

Courtland Van Rooten, mentor.

To each and all, my heartfelt thanks.

About the Glossary: A number of words and concepts in this book might be unfamiliar to American readers. As footnotes would have cluttered up the text, an alphabetical glossary, giving information to those eager for it while leaving others alone who might already know about the matter in question seemed preferable.

Regarding the Latin sentences and quotations: The men in this book were well educated. Their frequent use of Latin phrases, however, does not denote a desire to boast to each other about their schooling—nothing could have been further from their minds. Latin, in their day, was the idiom of the European intelligentsia, a common language from Paris to Krakow, from Stockholm to Palermo. Used for instant communication and inside jokes, it was an excellent time-saving device.

Should you be unfamiliar with Vergil's tongue, the Glossary is at your beck and call.

Live happily.

Cambridge, Massachusetts
Autumn 1978

The Moonclock

At Saint Mary's Church of the Minorite Brothers in Vienna. After bans duly called, Married: On 25 Decembris A.D. 1682, the Worthy Town Councilor and Burgher of Vienna, Jacobus Matthäus Schretter von Schrettenberg, aged 47 years, lawfully begotten son of the Late Georgius Schretter von Schrettenberg, Professor of Canon Law at the University ibidem, and of the Late Catharina Schretter von Schrettenberg, nata de Cischini, to Barbara Regina Cammerloherin, aged 20 years, Spinster, lawfully begotten daughter of the Late Christoph Cammerloher, former Private Secretary to His Eminence the Cardinal Archbishop of Salzburg, and of Brigitta Cammerloherin, nata Wiesner.

The Husband: Jacobus Schretter

The Bride: Barbara Schretter

The Copulant: Pater Anselmus Schallerbacher

IN WITNESS THEREOF:

For the Groom: Andreas von Liebenberg
                 Mayor of Vienna

                 Nicolaus Hocke, Doctor u.i.
                 Town Clerk of Vienna

For the Bride: Brigitta Cammerloherin, Widow,
                 Mother of the Bride

                 Leopold Kohlröser
                 *Captain in His Majesty's
                     Cavalry Regiment Caprara*

IN NOMINE DOMINI

Three Kings' Day, in the Year of the Lord 1683

Much-loved Thresl:

May God bless you in the New Year. I received your letter
and thank you for it. As my mother is back in Salzburg you
surely must have heard about the wedding by now: about
my veil getting caught in the carriage wheel, about the frozen organ pipes, how Pater Anselmus confused the rings so
that I had to stick mine on Jacob's little finger while I caught
his on my thumb (we exchanged them afterward), and how
she danced the gigue with the Mayor at the wedding party
and forgot all about her aching legs.

As soon as the dinner was served and the Mayor had
drunk a glass to our health, the men began to talk about war
and nothing else. It seems that the Turk is on the march
again because a twenty-year-old truce will be running out
this year. The Mayor said we should make ready for battle
and there will be not much time left, and Jacob said if only
the Emperor thought so too; but Master Hocke, the Town
Clerk whom Jacob had invited (he is short and thin and has
a voice which is high-pitched and husky all at once; you
might say a hoarse rooster), said that the Turk would never
dare come up to Vienna. At this the others laughed out loud
and kept arguing with him. At first I was somewhat scared,
for they sounded as if the Turk were already at our doors,
but then I got quite bored until the Mayoress said that such
was not fitting talk at a wedding dinner. The men said they
were sorry and as we had arrived at the sweets, the Mayor

rose and had the fiddlers strike up the *Franceschina*. I opened the dance with Jacob, who was a better dancer than I would have thought, considering his creaky joints, then the Mayor asked me for a courante (he only knows three steps and those are old-fashioned), and lastly I danced the gigue with your brother as, back home, I have done so often, save that this time I was sad, because I knew that he was to join his regiment down in Pressburg and will not be back until next year. He presented me with a bolt of green brocade—I never saw anything more precious, the stuff has birds and flowers woven into it—and your brother said he got it for me in Hungary from a Turkish merchant. From the Mayor I got twelve silver plates; on each is etched a story from the New Testament. I like the one with the Foolish Virgins best of all—one looks like you. The Mayoress brought forth a sewing box with golden scissors, a golden thimble, and many spools of red, blue, green, black, and white thread, but no needles. These, she said, I would have to buy myself, for giving needles means bad luck.

The party lasted until almost midnight. When it got time to retire my mother grew anxious. She embraced me several times and wept just as the Rainalterin did at Lisi's entering St. Ursula. Jacob told my mother to cheer up, that he was not about to eat me alive. Thereupon he said good night and went upstairs while the dancing was still going on. I went into my room where my mother and Margaret were waiting for me. They helped me out of my wedding dress, put me into a white nightgown, and went upstairs with me to the bedroom. They knocked at the door and Jacob opened, wearing a long, fur-lined dressing gown. As I entered I noticed in the light of four tall candles the canopied bed open and ready. It looked for all the world like a coffin. I was somewhat frightened, but Jacob was kind enough. "You must be tired," he said. "Let us go to sleep." So we climbed into the bed, I on the right side and he on the left; and he soon fell asleep—or at least he pretended—while I lay awake, keeping to my side of the bed and wishing I were back home in Salzburg.

I could hear the music from downstairs; Poldl surely was leading the courante with the Hallerin, who thinks she can dance. What was I doing in this bed, I thought, but for the Aigen Fair. Yet how was I to know that my father (God rest his soul) would not last more than six weeks afterward and that Poldl would come home so soon? Still, I do not think your brother would have wanted me. You know how he likes to say that he would not dream of getting married before he is at least lieutenant-general, and by now he is only captain and due back in his Pressburg garrison next week. They say (better tear up this page) that he keeps a Turkish girl there. However that may be, who says A must say B, so there I was in this bed. The Minorites' church clock struck one, then two, then three, the watchman calling out the hours. At last I slept some, only to wake again at the stroke of five. I was glad when morning came.

The following night I learned my *matrimonial duties.* If marriage were not a sacrament, I would have none of this business. It is silly and a little shameful. Yet one gets used to it. Jacob is never rude, neither is he awful looking, as are so many men of his age—he still has almost all of his hair and teeth, which is astonishing. Furthermore he hurt me not half as much as did Master Thurneysser (you remember him, the toothbreaker from Mondsee) when he pulled out my two back teeth.

This morning we walked to church through three feet of snow, with Xaver and Vitus digging a path ahead of us. Jacob suffers from gout, and it gets worse in the cold. My eyes hurt, I saw blue and yellow shadows in the snow, and later, in church, I could hardly make out the letters in my missal. Pater Anselmus, too, scared us with talk about the Turks. He said they may come up from Hungary and made us pray against them. I do hope they stay where they belong.

The Danube is all frozen. Yesterday Jacob and I were driving by the Red Tower Gate and watched the skating for a while. There were many folk, among them two fat girls attempting to do Threes and Eights. Luckily for them they were all padded around, for they kept falling on their rears. Jacob laughed and said they were to be commended for trying so hard, but I said they could try till doomsday the way they were doing it and that I could show them a thing or two if only he would buy me a pair of skates and let me go down. Yet he would have none of it. He thinks I may be pregnant and fears that I could come to grief (which God may prevent). Still, it made me angry, so I said, "Let us go home. If I am not allowed to skate I do not care to watch."

Last night I went to St. Anne's for the Vigil and brought clothes and soup for the beggars there. They said that some old folks in the almshouse froze to death, and I saw Sister Agnes taking care of two boys with scurvy heads. An old woman said this comes from lard dripping on someone's head, but I think this is nonsense. Those two looked as if they had not had any lard to eat for three or four years.

I forgot to tell you that Master Hocke gave me a gilt-and-leather–bound book — the Almanac and Perpetual Calendar of the famous Dr. Colerus, with many blank pages after each month, to enter all things necessary for thrifty house-keeping, as he said, and above all my expenses.

Jacob gives me 90 florins a week, which should do for food, firewood, alms, and servants' wages; but I think that if I want, say, a new dress or bedcover I will have to ask him. He does not spend much on himself, wears a coat that is at least ten years old; yet the other day I saw him pay 20 florins for an old sheepskin-bound book without even bargaining. Maybe I can skimp some on my 90 florins — a kreuzer here, ten kreuzer there — to have a little money of my own so I can pay the seamstress to make me a dress out of your brother's green silk.

Recommend me to your father and your mother and wish them a Blessed New Year for me.

Your loving friend,
Barbara

❧❦❧

MICHAEL KIRNSPERGER, DEACON OF ST. MARY'S AT INNSBRUCK, TO JACOB SCHRETTER, IN VIENNA

This January 7, Anno Salutis Nostrae 1683

Amice dilectissime:

First of all receive my well-wishing for the New Year. May it bring God's blessing to you and also the heir for whom you have been praying. A word of caution, though, if you will forgive an old friend: Do not show too much impatience with your wife, should she as yet not show any sign of being with child, but give her a little mead to drink after dinner. If she gets stomach pains this would indicate that she is pregnant. If not, you may have to wait a little longer. And do not forget: She is young, has to learn many things. The *Oeconomia* is a great and difficult art. No one can say to have learned everything about it, not even during a long lifetime. Teach her diligently, commend her often—virtus laudata crescit. I know that you will always protect her, that you will never beat or curse her.

Here, however, comes to mind a necessary item which I want to share with you:

The Devil has afflicted the poor female sex with vanity. Often a wife will pester her husband for jewelry, for clothes of the newest cut, and for a big, stately house. This is caused by the little word the Devil whispered to Eve, namely: "Eritis sicut Deus." To this day women have not digested this little word. That is why many a husband calls his wife fundi sui calamitatem, the misfortune of his moneybag. A man has to explain to his wife that money which is to be spent on food ought not be thrown away for rags of silk and velvet which will be torn and threadbare within the year. Nor should money be squandered on a heap of stones. Far better to have a small, but well-stocked house than to sit in a big place with an empty barn and a ledger full of debts.

On re-reading your letter I see that I almost forgot to give you the desired recipe for the gout medicine:

Gout remedy:

Whenever you feel arthritis coming into your fingers or feet, take two good handfuls of horse manure. Put it into an earthen pot. Pour red wine over it. Close the pot, bury it in cow manure, and leave it there for eight days. Then boil the mixture and drain the liquid. Drench pieces of linen in it and wrap them around your fingers and toes, wherever you hurt. It is a very quick remedy, the Prince Elector's Councilor has also used it. It stinks terribly, but pray do not mind it, for Evil has to be driven out by Evil.

Recommending you to God's goodness, I remain

Your affectionate friend,
Michael Kirnsperger

✦§✦

BRIGITTA WIDOW CAMMERLOHERIN, IN SALZBURG, TO HER DAUGHTER, BARBARA SCHRETTER, IN VIENNA

On January 7, in the Year of the Lord 1683

Dear Daughter:

I know that the Taxis Mail is quite slow these days, but I would welcome a letter from you—I am worried as to how you are faring.

Yesterday, Three Kings' Day, was frighteningly cold. Now the day is longer by a rooster's pace and this is good, for much work has to be done. Firewood has to be brought down from the mountain in the sleigh right now, since later it would be much harder to move about in all the mud and melting snow.

Yesterday the Archbishop read the Great Mass himself. The church was crowded but still cold; I could see white steam coming out of everybody's mouth as if they all were smoking tobacco. Many had their money stolen. The Mass was a new one, written by an Italian and sung by all the boys. They had the sniffles.

I walked home with the Kohlröserin, who told me that Thresl does not want to get married; she even said to her mother that she'd rather take the veil than become Straihamer's wife. Thresl is making her parents wretched because they had promised her hand to him, but you know what a headstrong girl she is. She might enter St. Ursula just for spite or — God forbid — come to a worse end.

The lads had to hack the ice in the river and bring it home in buckets; it melts very slowly. The firewood is frozen outside and damp inside, and we can hardly cook because the fireplace in the kitchen smokes all the time. So we drink some good spirits to keep us warm until it pleases God to let it thaw.

Be good to your husband and show him respect. He deserves it. I grant you, marriage to a much older man is not always pleasant (neither is being married to a young one, for that matter), but a woman has to make the best of her lot and yours is indeed a happy one. Jacob is a good, decent man; there are not many like him around nowadays. Make him a clean and cheerful home. His first wife, God rest her soul, was not much of a housewife. Therefore you will be spared the litany so many second wives have to hear from their husbands — "No one could make better roast duck than my poor Lisi," "Why can't you make cheese cake the way Crescence did?" "My Lori, may she rest in peace, would always have the bedwarmers ready"—and no end to it. By the way, do not ever use bedwarmers. They can set straw mattresses on fire very quickly, as happened yesterday at St. Roch's orphanage, where the Prior's bedwarmer had his mattress and bed in flames before you could yell "Fire!" Half the Priory burned down, and while most of the children escaped, two or three of them suffocated in the smoke.

But to come back to your husband: Be friendly, overlook his weaknesses, and do not quarrel with him over trifles. Stand your ground quietly and pleasantly whenever much is at stake. He will respect you for it.

Do not trust the servants. Keep everything locked and always carry the keys on your belt, lest things be stolen by evil and untrustworthy folk. (Nowadays the world is full of them.) Check your servants' beds and straw mattresses from time to time, and look into the far corners of kitchen and pantry. There you might, likely as not, come upon some secret treasure trove and find rye, grits, eggs, oats, cheese, bread, and what not hidden away. You also should search their chests and drawers whenever they are not around. Keep a skeleton key handy for this purpose, but be sure not to let such a key lie about lest the servants pay you back in your own kind.

Do not grumble if sometimes you have more work to do than your servants have. After all, they have to work for someone else, while you can enjoy that which is your own, thanks to a good husband.

Although you must never be too familiar with your servants, you should treat them fairly and give them decent food. You also have to allow them enough time to rest and sleep.

Serving men and scullery maids, however, should not talk together or loaf around in dark corners, for then it often happens that at a time when one needs every pair of hands for work, one has to have a christening or a wedding. Therefore, whenever you see that they are getting ready for nesting, get rid of them as fast as you can. However, if you have among your servants a lad and a girl who want to get married in all honesty, then prepare a neat little wedding for them so that these poor folk, too, can set up a homestead and keep house.

Old Sabina Wannerin died yesterday. They have not buried her yet—the ground in St. Peter's churchyard is frozen three feet deep. They put her in the coffin and carried it upstairs to the threshing floor, where she will keep until the thaw sets in.

God bless you.

Your affectionate mother,
Brigitta Cammerloherin, Widow

◄§§►

BARBARA SCHRETTER, IN VIENNA, TO THERESIA KOHLRÖSER, IN
SALZBURG

This January 13, A.D. 1683

Dearest Thresl:
The Taxis Mail (on horseback) made it to Vienna through the heavy snow. Yet there was no letter from you. This made me feel quite sad for I had looked forward to hearing

from you. So I am now sitting down at my new secretary that Jacob has bought me. It is made of rosewood and has many tiny drawers. I don't know yet what to put into them. It also has a secret compartment which you open by pressing a hidden spring.

As I said, we are having lots of snow. There is a little hill right in front of our house; that is, the street goes down rather steeply toward the Löwel Bastion, and children and also older folk are having a good time with their sleighs. As I watched from the window some of them beckoned to me to come down and sleigh with them, but Jacob forbade it, again, because he thinks I might get hurt and he does not even know whether I am with child yet. Moreover, our street is so short, one could not go fast even if one wished to; he should have seen us coming down the Kapuzinerberg with your brother. Do you go sledding these days? With whom?

Tomorrow there will be a big sleigh carousel with torches in the Castle Square. Jacob is quite angry about this for the Town is to pay half of the expenses and he says that in these cold winter days the money is needed for the poor homeless who are the Town's wards. (He does not think much of the Emperor. Thus he will most likely not take me to watch the pageant.)

They say it is truly splendid and that the Archbishop's Horse Ballet looks like a county fair beside it. Perhaps I can get Margaret to set out for Vespers an hour earlier, and we can climb on the Castle Bastion. One has a good view from there, so we could at least see the entrance parade and still be in time for alms at St. Anne's. And even if we were too late, Sister Agnes should not grumble; after all, I go there three times a week and who knows how long I would have to wait for the next Sleigh Carousel?

It is cold indeed. I am wearing three underskirts and heavy woolen stockings, and I also bought some for Cathrin and the other servant girls. The windows are covered with ice flowers. Margaret likes them for it makes window washing easier and I like them because they show so many wondrous shapes—of flowers, leaves, grass, even thistles. "I wonder," I said to Jacob, "how those frozen water drops know about the shapes of thistles and flowers, since they so earnestly strive to counterfeit them." Jacob said, "Who knows, perhaps they want to be alive, as do all things under God's eye. So they do what they can for a short winter's day even though the sun will melt them soon, that sun which is so kind to their green brothers."

Margaret, who had overheard him saying this, made a face at me, but I liked what Jacob had said.

I do like him, truly. He is pleasant company, at least, he is whenever he is free of his gout (which does not happen often these days, for the cold worsens the affliction). Last night he was in great pain but when I asked him whether he wanted a cataplasm of warm wine, he waxed impatient, saying the gout cramps his joints, but not his mouth, and that I may be sure that he would tell me if he needed anything, and to leave him alone. I rather would have him scream and yell instead of making me guess his every want. Still, when he is in a good mood, he can make you laugh most heartily. But he dislikes gossip, most of all the bits and pieces Margaret brings home from the market and from talking with the neighbors' servants. He does not want me to repeat those things to him. The other day Margaret said he should be grateful to her for keeping her ears open, and he replied that he would be even more grateful if she kept her mouth shut. This made me laugh, but it also annoyed me, for after this Margaret was cross and said it was all my fault, why couldn't I have waited to marry. Now here we sit in Vienna and she was of no mind to run my household forever. This happens often. Whenever Margaret has a quarrel with Jacob he gets the better of her and she takes it out on me.

Jacob does not care about clothes. He wears a coat that is easily ten years old. I am somewhat ashamed in church, all the more as he could look so much better. Last week the Duke of Lorraine paid a visit to Vienna and was received at Town Hall by the Mayor, the Rector of the University, and all the Town Councilors—you should have seen Jacob in his black robe with the ruffle and the chain around his neck and shoulders—he cut a handsome figure. Afterward, when I asked why would he not dress a little more carefully and after a newer fashion he answered, "No, thank you, I am not a clotheshanger," but there he is wrong. He *is* a clotheshanger, what with his thin, bony shoulders. A scarecrow, says Margaret, but that is going too far.

As for my marriage duties. They are not easy. However, I know that I must get used to them. Thank God he does not want this every night, and thank God he gets contented rather quickly and falls asleep on the spot. I wish I could fall asleep as promptly, but I lie awake for hours with my chin quivering and I cannot hold it steady and I feel as if I had swallowed a stone. At such hours it looks to me as if no one cared about me, not even the Good Lord. Yet I know it is sinful to say such things, for without God's will no hair falls from your head. So I say my prayers and by Angelus I fall asleep until Margaret wakes me to go to early Mass and then I have a headache. Maybe all this will go away as soon as I am with child. At least Margaret says so. One thing, though, makes this business somewhat easier. Jacob never draws the bed curtains closed and he also often leaves a window open, for he says fresh air has never killed anybody. At first I was very much ashamed to have to fulfill my marriage duties in the light of a full moon, but now I just close my eyes. Jacob says that a sacrament does not ask of you to choke. I could not sleep with drawn curtains anymore.

Jacob also insists I take a bath once a week. I use an old washtub in the kitchen, and Margaret grumbles about it, for it takes at least eight buckets of water, which must be fetched from the well — now we melt the snow, half of it being heated in the big kettle over the kitchen fire. It is very pleasant and I can hardly understand how, back home, I could make do with a bath every three weeks only. We use lots of lye for the soap — too much, says Margaret — and we scent it with cloves.

Jacob likes his hot baths. They help him against his gout, he says. The other day he fell into a dispute about it with Pater Anselmus, who had come for a visit. The Pater said that the Empress never bathed and that bathing so often was a heathenish custom. "Quite right," Jacob replied, "and the Roman heathens bathed not once a week in an old washtub, but every day in a big basin hewn from red marble and supported by bronze lion's claws," and, he said, when he was living in Italy he did that too. One feels wondrously well afterward, and Pater Anselmus should try it once, Jacob said. At this the Pater got mad, for his rule forbids all vanity of the body. Yet Jacob was right, I think, for when the Pater got up to take his leave I spotted three lice marching down the back of the chair on which he had sat. I could not wait for the Pater to go so I could squash them before they crawled into the seat cushion, but he kept talking and when he left at last it was too late. We washed the seat cushion with camphor and vinegar, but it ruined the embroidery and the lice kept hiding.

Now whenever I go to confession the Pater asks me whether I had bathed and if so he gives me a whole rosary to recite.

Pater Anselmus also asks me often whether I have been obedient. Then he falls asleep in his confessional. I keep on talking, and whenever I pause he wakes up and says: "That is a mean thing to do, do not do it anymore, and pray three rosaries." If I told him that I just killed my husband, he'd probably say, "That is a mean thing to do, do not do it anymore, and pray three rosaries." But I would never play such a prank on the Pater; one must not joke about such things, truly not, all the more after what happened last week — they hanged the Kuglerin, our neighbor, for having poisoned her husband. She was pregnant when they got her, so they could not hang her as long as she was with child; but they kept her in the dungeon, and it was there that she was delivered. The Hutterin (the midwife) said to Margaret afterward, "Too bad. So many women die in childbirth and the Kuglerin had to come through just to be hanged." She had a baby boy—they put him in the orphanage. Margaret said, "It serves her right. Why did she insist on making Kugler's supper herself? With a cook and six servants she could have found some other way." I go to the orphanage often to bring them food and clothes, and last week they showed me the Kugler child. He is a handsome little boy. I told Sister Sperantia to get him a wet nurse and I would pay for the woman (they only cost two florins a week).

Marie Stifl, the cobbler's widow, died yesterday. When they opened her will they found she had left all her things to her five children, save a little medallion with her picture, which was to be given to one Jörg Krainer, of whom no one had ever heard. In her will she calls him "her betrothed until copulation." The family was angry, but Jacob, to whom they came to complain, ordered them to turn over the medallion to the old man. Margaret said too bad the cobbler had lasted so long—Marie had been a widow for only two years—and that I am fortunate indeed to have married a man so much older than myself. I might become a widow before too long, she said, and then could have some fun in life. I am also spared a mother-in-law, she added. I was angry at her for her rudeness for I do like Jacob, and furthermore I do not even have a medallion with my picture inside. And if I had one, to whom would I leave it?

Margaret quarrels with Jacob all the time. Yesterday it was about the garbage, which he wants to be heaped in the yard and burned once a week instead of being thrown into the street. He says in Rome they have come to keeping the streets quite clean, and he was going to make the Mayor issue a City Ordinance, forbidding garbage heaps outside the houses. As soon as he said "Rome," Margaret was mollified, as you can well believe. She likes the Italians from her campaign days. They were pleasant, she says, and cared more for women and loot than for killing everybody in sight.

Jacob does not like Margaret to rule the house so thoroughly and keeps telling me that I should begin to oversee the servants myself. This means kitchen, house, and cellar. There is so much to do, that at night I am weary.

I am pretty much locked in here. The neighbors' wives are all older, and I see them only in church. I cannot even go for a walk right now because of all the snow. They have not held a market in days; our food comes from hawkers' back baskets and is being hauled in through the window.

I wish I had my spinet. Do you still keep up your singing lessons? Please give Signor Pasquali my regards, and tell him I would be happy now if I could practice his figured bass. Maybe Jacob will buy me a spinet; I would be content with a single keyboard.

I do hear music, it is true, aside from Mass on Sunday: Lots of street fiddlers and rote players come before our windows and play in the cold with their frostbitten fingers—sometimes they are quite bloody. We have a big pot full of soup going the whole day to feed those poor folk—they say our soup is much better than the stuff they get at St. Anne's—Margaret thinks it a waste, but Jacob insisted and she gave in.

We are having trouble with the cesspool. It is frozen and full and we have to empty the slop jars into the street. Thank God it is so cold that you cannot smell anything yet. Jacob says that as soon as the ice melts he will have all cesspools and slop-jar refuse covered with quicklime.

18

I am not yet with child.

Dearest Thresl, write to me. Cathrin is taking this to the Taxis Mail. Pray tell my mother that I kiss her hands and that I will write to her tomorrow. (Right now I do not have the heart to write to her about the things she wants to know, such as my linen, silver, crockery, salted meats, pickles, jelly, servants' wages, and Jacob's religion.)

Your loving friend,
Barbara

The old Duchess of Rohan's chambermaid will sew my green brocade dress—she hires herself out all over town and gets 25 florins for an outfit. I think I can manage this. She was beside herself when she saw the stuff, said the Duchess would make eyes as big as saucers if she could see it, and that it was fit for a queen.

ALMANAC—BARBARA SCHRETTER'S HAND

Sister Agnes' Cough Medicine

One nutmeg One pint of water
One tablespoon of honey One pinch of ground cloves
Boil it all together, let it cool some, gargle with it, and
drink it.

THERESIA KOHLRÖSER, IN SALZBURG, TO BARBARA SCHRETTER,
IN VIENNA

This January 25, A.D. 1683

Dearest Barbara:

I hasten to answer your letter. Your mother came to dinner
the other night, as did Dr. Straihamer. He had fetched her
in a small sleigh—he had one horse hitched to it—and
drove it standing behind her seat, the old fool. My mother
and father did whatever they could to do him great honor
and wished me to be at my very best, but I soon retired with
a headache. I swear to you that I will not marry him; he can
wait until doomsday for my *matrimonial duties*. I'd rather
become an old maid and sit and spin for the rest of my life.
Straihamer brought a kind of spyglass with him and made
everybody look through it at drops of water. You can see
many little worms wriggling around. He says he cannot wait
for the next Plague for he is sure that he will find many of
those beasts in the blood of the sick. The Plague on *him*.

It is too bad that your husband would not let you skate. We—the Lechner Ploni, a few others, and I—went to St. Gilgen in a sleigh and skated on the lake.

We had slaughtered some pigs during the last quarter of the moon. The food came in handy, for a fortnight ago St. Roch's orphanage burned down, and there was no water to put out the fire, everything being frozen. Some of the poor little souls perished in the flames, but most of them could run out. The townsfolk took them into their houses, as is everyone's Christian duty. We have two, a girl and a boy, whose names are Toni and Joseph. He is fourteen, which is too old for a choirboy and too young for a soldier. Perhaps my brother can take Joseph with him in a year or so.

When my mother found they had lice, she washed their heads with sulphur. They yelled as if possessed by the Devil, but the lice would not all go away.

I am pleased that you liked the green silk so much. (I saw it. Poldl had it with him on his last furlough and we all thought that it would go well indeed with your hair.)

Signor Pasquali comes once a week, we sing for half an hour, and then he tells me everything that goes on at the Castle. There will be a great Wirtschaft on Rose Monday—it will take hard work to bring my mother around so she will let me go, for at first she will most certainly forbid it.

Take good care of yourself and see to it that your husband buys you a fur coat, since he makes you walk to church.

Your Foolish Virgin,
Thresl

BARBARA SCHRETTER, IN VIENNA, TO HER MOTHER, THE
WIDOW BRIGITTA CAMMERLOHERIN, IN SALZBURG

Candlemas Day, A.D. 1683

My Dear Mother:

I received your letter and thank you for it. Do not worry
yourself. I strive to do my best and will heed all your advice.
You may be sure that I will not give any keys away except to
Margaret, who helps me very much in overseeing the household. I am indeed grateful to you for having let her come
with me. My husband did not like her in the beginning, as
you know, but the other day, when the surgeon was sick, it
was she who bled Jacob. She did it well, far better than the
surgeon, he said, and though he says she is an old witch, he
does not mind her so much anymore.

We bought a whole barrel of eels caught in the Danube
under the ice, and put them into vinegar. They are kept in
the cellar so we will always have a good dish ready if unex-
pected guests should arrive. We also bought a barrel of herrings, which Margaret and Cathrin strung up in the smoke
house.

Next week we will have to thaw some snow for washing
so we can begin changing our bedding again every four
weeks. After Ash Wednesday Jacob wants to go to see how
things are in his garden at the Löwel Bastion.

I kiss your hands and pray that God may bless and keep
you.

Your obedient daughter,
Barbara

BARBARA SCHRETTER, IN VIENNA, TO THERESIA KOHLRÖSER, IN
SALZBURG

On February 25, St. Matthew's Day, A.D. 1683

My Dear Friend Thresl:

Forgive me, pray, for having taken so long in answering your
letter. (It came the day after I had complained that you did
not write.) Jacob has been plagued by his gout and the
housework took much time every day. Now the weather has
let up a bit, as Margaret predicted:

> St. Matthew breaks the ice.
> If there's none
> He makes some.

This year he certainly had no trouble finding enough ice
to break.

Last Monday—on Rose Monday—Jacob took me to a
dance at Court. He bought himself a new wig, but none for
me. He said if one has hair long enough to sit on one's
plaits, one does not need a wig. Besides, he said, fashion
does not call for ladies' wigs and I should wear a fontange as
do other women of standing. What does he know of fashion, I thought, and then I asked him for money to buy a few
lengths of lace. He gave me 10 florins, which was not nearly
enough. I wanted to ask for more, but Margaret winked at
me and shook her head, to make me close my mouth. As
soon as my husband had left she said, "No trouble. We will
cut a few lengths of lace from your bridal veil and use the
money to buy ribbons." And that is what we did, and even

saved 5 florins. (I do hope my mother will not ask to see my bridal veil again for quite a while.) Margaret made me a fontange from the lace and the ribbons and it turned out well. I wore the green brocade dress, and beforehand I took a bath in rose water. I also treated my face against freckles. The recipe came out of Margaret's little book—it must be at least a hundred years old—which is called *Quodlibeticus.* Jacob says it is full of nonsense. He does not like it too well when we use the prescriptions from it. Yet he does not know that the spiced hot wine he likes so much for his night cup is also made from a *Quodlibeticus* recipe.

Here is the freckles water, should you want it:

Take fennel; crush and boil it. Add allspice and goosefat. Let it cool, and wash your face with it. It will take the freckles away, though not all of them. Also: If you wash your hair, first spread egg white all over your face and neck so that sharp soap will not bite into your skin. Rinse your hair in vinegar, or better, in lemon juice.

As I said, I wore my green brocade dress to the Court Dance. Many guests were already in the Great Hall at the Castle when we arrived. It was quite hot, so that I almost suffocated and was glad that I had a fresh pomander with me. The chandeliers made it hotter and kept dripping on my dress. Jacob introduced me to some ladies of the nobility and also presented a few gentlemen to me, two old Italians in particular. One of them was Ambassador Magalotti, about fifty, tall and thin, with a hooked nose and twinkling eyes. He kissed my hands and said something in Italian to Jacob which made them both smile and I was a little embarrassed because my Italian is none too good. As you know, all

I know are the arias Signor Pasquali taught us. The other gentleman also was thin, but short and all dried up. His name was Cavaliere Ricasoli. Both of them said that if they were twenty years younger they would vie for dances with me, but now, Cavaliere Ricasoli added, he thought that I would prefer another escort, namely, his son. He himself, the Ambassador, and Jacob intended to sit and have a good talk.

The young Cavaliere Ricasoli came over to us just then. He is tall and has gray eyes under dark eyebrows and danced with me almost the whole time. I wondered whether he knew that my fontange was homemade and was ashamed that I had almost no jewelry except my pearl earrings and my gold necklace. He found my Italian very good and laughed when I explained to him that the little I knew I had learned from my music master and so I could only talk in recitatives. He told me about a painter named Tiziano who, he said, would have liked my hair. The Emperor owns a few pictures painted by this man, I hear; I would be curious to see them.

Then everything came to a standstill as the Emperor and the Empress made their entrance. The Emperor has aged since I saw him last year at the Corpus Christi procession. His lower jaw is so long and sticks out so much that I do not see how he can talk, let alone eat. His color is pale and he limps.

The Empress is thin and has a pockmarked face. They say she refuses to cover her pockmarks with even a little paint, because, she says, God intended her to look pockmarked; otherwise He would not have sent the pox upon her.

Afterward we danced some more and I ate ice sherbet—it was very pleasant in the heat. Everybody was sweating, but I did not mind, for Cavaliere Ricasoli is a great and excellent dancer. At the Kehraus some ladies and gentlemen even formed a little circle around us—they were exhausted—to watch us dance the last gigue.

As we left there was a great confusion of runners, torches, and coaches in the courtyard. Vitus was not there and neither was the Ricasolis' driver, so the Ambassador offered to take us all home. They called for his carriage, but it took a while before it came forward. We stood under the Swiss Gate and it was very cold after the stuffy ballroom.

"What an ungodly hour," Jacob said. "We might as well stay up for early Mass." "Not that ungodly," said the Ambassador. "It is only half past three." When we wondered how he could tell the hour so accurately, he answered, "By the moonclock." I thought this to be a joke, but no, he pointed up to the Castle Tower which has a sundial on the front side, its rod now casting a moonshade, but it showed twelve o'clock. Jacob said that such a moonclock would be right only a few nights out of the whole year, and you would have to do some heavy reckoning at that. Meanwhile the carriage had drawn up and we mounted. We had to squeeze some, and I found myself sitting between Jacob and the young Cavaliere.

Jacob and the Ambassador talked very eagerly about the figuring of the moonclock. The old Signor de' Ricasoli laughed and said that all their mathematics would be of little avail, for by the time they had their reckoning done, the clock would be farther ahead, as the moon runs very fast over the firmament. But the young Cavaliere pressed my hand a little and said very softly (nobody heard him in the clatter of the wheels) that he liked the thought of such a clock which showed only the enchanted hours of a few nights. He kept my hand in his and when I tried to withdraw it he held it a little tighter, which meant that I could not pull it back without making a commotion. So I just sat still.

When we arrived at the house, Jacob invited them for a night cup, but I excused myself and went to bed, for I felt that they wanted to have some talking and drinking among themselves.

Around ten the next night, on Shrove Tuesday, we heard a very agreeable music coming from the street. I hurried to the window, and there down below stood the young Cavaliere Ricasoli with two fiddlers. He was playing a lute and wore a mask since it was still Carnival, but I recognized him on the spot. They were serenading me. Jacob had already gone to bed, he had had a bad, gouty day, and was a little angry because they had awakened him. He told Margaret— half in jest—to empty the slop jar on them and that he would gladly pay the fine. But I know that he liked the music, for he lingered at the window, and all the neighbors looked out of theirs and clapped after every song. They were still singing when suddenly the big bell from St. Stephen's rang in Ash Wednesday and I had to go to bed.

In the early morning I went to Mass with Margaret. The Cavaliere was at the church door. He greeted me and as we entered he took off his glove and offered me the Holy Water as is the custom in Italy. We went forward to the altar and he knelt beside me as Pater Anselmus drew the ashen cross on everybody's forehead.

Carnival is over. I wish the Cavaliere would go back to Florence, for that is where he comes from. And then again I wish he would stay.

Recommend me to your father and to your mother. (Did she let you go to the Wirtschaft? Let me know.)

My husband says that Dr. Straihamer's spyglass will not show him a thing in the blood of Plague-sick folk because the Plague comes from foul air and uncleanliness. He also says that Straihamer is a Theophrastian quack.

> Many good wishes from
> Your affectionate friend,
> Barbara

FROM MARGARET'S QUODLIBETICUS

To Dye Your Hair The Way You Fancy It

First of all, smear your hair with bear's grease, three or four times over. Dissolve some lye in water. If you want your hair yellow, put ground saffron into the lye; if you want it black, put ashes and dry vine leaves into it; if you want it white, add sulphur.

JACOB SCHRETTER TO MONSIGNOR MICHAEL KIRNSPERGER,
DEACON AT ST. MARY'S IN INNSBRUCK

February 25, Thursday after Ash Wednesday, A.D. 1683

Dear and Honored Friend:

Greetings.

Pray do not fear that I may treat my wife too severely. Acta loquuntur: On Rose Monday there was a dance at Court and I took her there. The expense was considerable—I needed a new wig. I never was much one for dancing and now my gout keeps me from it more than ever. So I sat with Ricasoli and—read and marvel!—Magalotti (he is now Cosimo's Ambassador here, what a pleasant surprise) under a dripping chandelier and talked of old times at the Crusca, while Barbara danced to her heart's content. I did not begrudge her this, since she is young and this might have been her last ball for quite a while, for I hope and pray that she may soon be with child.

Ricasoli and Magalotti send you their affectionate greetings. They are busier than ever at the Cimento, it seems. Redi is now concerned with insects and has the whole Pitti buzzing with bugs. Magalotti wants to know whether you would like to read his Refutatio per scientiam of some half-witted atheist theory.

Starhemberg spotted us and joined us for a while. He worries that we may have to go to war with France and with the Sultan at the same time and wants to conscribe men for moat digging. The Emperor is less concerned about these matters. He holds that we are still at truce with the Turk and lavishes money (that should be spent at rebuilding our crumbling bastions) on a new opera at which he intends to play (an indubitably excellent) continuo.

Would that Mars had favored him a little more and the Muses a little less—we'd all fare a whole sight better.

Their Majesties presided over the Ball. The Empress is pregnant again. It is rather astonishing, what with her fasts and flagellations. This will make the ninth time.

Keep me in your thoughts, dear friend, and say a prayer for my hopes. The Emperor, whose gout is worse than mine, will, God granting, have nine children within the year. Est in votis.

Salve atque vale.

Your devoted friend,
Jacob Schretter

◄◊◊►

THERESIA KOHLRÖSER, IN SALZBURG, TO BARBARA SCHRETTER,
IN VIENNA

This March 4, A.D. 1683

Dearest Barbara

I thank you for your recent letter. I am glad that the dance pleased you so much. As for your Cavaliere, *believe me*— better let well enough alone.

Poldl wrote from Eisenstadt. He will be on furlough for three days and might come to visit you and your husband sometime soon.

Pray forgive this short letter; nothing much is happening here.

I embrace you.

Your affectionate friend,
Thresl

◄§ℰ►

BARBARA SCHRETTER, IN VIENNA, TO HER FRIEND, THERESIA
KOHLRÖSER, IN SALZBURG

This March 10, in the Year of the Lord 1683

Dear Thresl:

Many thanks for your letter. Though short, it pleased me very much to hear from you. You say that nothing much is happening in Salzburg. Here we had a few commotions.

A fortnight ago the night watchman got drunk, fell over his lantern, and set himself afire. It happened in the Minorites' Alley, not far from our house. We had heard him call out the ninth hour, and Jacob had remarked on the man's heavy tongue and had even joked about it, but all of a sudden we heard a scream. We hurried to the window and saw him burning like a torch. Everybody ran out into the street and threw snow at him. At the end we quenched the flames, but he was badly burned. Margaret ran for the apothecary, who treated the burns with horse manure and bloodwater, but the man died a few hours later. The following Sunday Pater Anselmus preached long and loud against drunkenness. He called it a Friendly Devil, a Sweet Poison, a

Shipwreck of Virtue, the Mother of Sadness, the Root of All Sickness, the Joy of the Devil, the Capital in Vice Land, and many things more. Yet I believe that the night watchman drank spirits merely to keep warm, for it was bitter cold for walking to and fro and calling out the hours. We have now a new night watchman. He blows a horn, awakening me every hour.

A week later they brought Vitus home with badly frozen feet. He had been conscripted for digging at the city walls. Count Starhemberg is making many people work at the walls for long hours, for in the spring the Turk might be on the move (God forbid).

The apothecary came again. His name is Schabeyssen; he is short and fat and wears a wig that is almost as high as a sugar hat. He told Cathrin to fetch some ice water in a bucket. When she brought it he had Vitus sit on a chair, grabbed his feet and stuck them into the ice water. (The feet looked yellow and brown.) It must have hurt him cruelly for he yelled and it took three people to restrain him, Xaver, Margaret, and Cathrin. Vitus kept on yelling and the apothecary forced a few spoonfuls of anis liquor into him. The second and third day he did not yell anymore; he said that he had lost all feeling in his feet, when they stuck them again into the ice water. The fourth day Schabeyssen smeared his legs and feet with a liniment of oil and crushed spiders. He did not get gangrene, God be praised, but kept his feet.

When Jacob heard about this (he was at the Town Hall when Schabeyssen came) he said that Vitus's healthy nature got the better of Schabeyssen's cure and that this quack should only be allowed to bleed his patients, but not to try his hellish salves on them.

Yesterday my spinet arrived from Salzburg. Jacob had sent for it as a surprise for me. I was quite touched, for the Taxis Mail must have billed him heavily for it. Jacob is not always cheerful because the gout is often upon him, but he is a good man.

I will now go and play some music; perhaps I can remember the Kehraus gigue they played at the Ball.

May God keep you in good cheer. Write to me when you have the time.

Your affectionate friend,
Barbara

❦

MONSIGNOR MICHAEL KIRNSPERGER, DEACON OF ST. MARY'S IN
INNSBRUCK, TO JACOB SCHRETTER, IN VIENNA

This March 20, A.S.N. 1683

Dear and Honorable Friend:

It gladdened my heart to hear from you and from our old friends. I wished I had all three of you at my table, doing honor to a well-roasted capon and to a '79 Montepulciano. Pray tell Magalotti to send me his treatise forthwith, for I am a great admirer of his Ciceronian style. As for the subject, I hold that he wasted his eloquence. It should suffice to place any atheist before a flowering tree to make him recant his silly utterances and praise the Optimus Artifex.

Here in the mountains, spring is coming slowly, and with what joy do I await it. The older I get the more eager I am for the fair season to return. Truly the Lord smiles at us and at all nature through the warmth of His sun. He gives back health and strength to man. The beasts go back to the pastures, the birds sing in the air and in the trees, thanking Our Lord that He has brought them back into the light. Even old bookworms like me feel like taking long walks. In short, the world now cuts a truly fine figure, showing us a picture of Life Eternal as, before their Fall, Adam and Eve had in Paradise.

Let us pray that Turks and pestilence will spare us this year. I was somewhat frightened by your mention of His Grace Count Starhemberg's concern. You have your garden outside the walls—God keep it safe from those heathens.

If you plant by the moon and by the stars, keep in mind to plant three days before the full moon and to graft three days before the new moon.

Give my greetings to your excellent wife.

Salutem in Christo

Your friend,
Michael Kirnsperger

•§§•

JACOB SCHRETTER, IN VIENNA, TO MONSIGNOR MICHAEL
KIRNSPERGER, DEACON OF ST. MARY'S IN INNSBRUCK

This Fourth Aprilis, *A.D. 1683*

My Dear and Learned Friend:
Your letters always fill me with great pleasure. Yes, spring has come, God be praised. Let us pray that this year will be merciful to all of us.

In February Starhemberg held conscriptions for work on the walls. However, this was no more than a drop in the bucket—the bastions are crumbling and need to be fortified from the ground. Starhemberg tries his utmost to convince His Majesty of this state of affairs, but Leopold still thinks that the Turkish Truce will hold and that they never would dare to lay siege to us. Est in votis. My Vitus got considerably damaged while shoveling at the walls; his feet almost froze off, but he is a strong lad and recovered with the help of God rather than the efforts of the apothecary.

This disciple of Aesculapius, Schabeyssen by name, was one day consulted by me about some medicine against gout and against colic, for, as you know, I happen to be plagued by both those evils. The recipe he gave me calls for three or four skulls of such persons as have been hanged but not buried. Schabeyssen says it is important that the skulls be from men. (As if a skull ever had stated whether it had been a man's or a woman's.) His remedy against gout calls for the shinbones of a hanged man. Non probatum est. I think not much of this necromancy, which is an unholy superstition and displeasing to God.

I have bought some more land to extend my garden outside the walls and intend to plant a few fruit trees.

There is much joy in my garden, as one indeed can see God's blessing in all things that come forth from the Earth. Whenever I look at a tree, a flower, or an herb, I feel like singing a *Te Deum*.

Include me in your prayers, dear friend.

Salve atque vale.

Your devoted friend,
Jacobus Schretter

35

BRIGITTA CAMMERLOHER, WIDOW IN SALZBURG, TO HER
DAUGHTER, BARBARA SCHRETTER, IN VIENNA

This April 17, in the Year of the Lord 1683

Dear Daughter:

Forgive me for not having written to you for some time. My legs gave me great trouble, and I had to stay in bed for almost three weeks. They bled me with leeches, also gave me a broth of leeches to drink, but it did not seem to help much. Another surgeon came and said I had hairworms. He put my legs into a basin of warm water, held some old wool against the broken skin, and waited for the worms to come out. But none came. So he made a kind of lye with burned straw, saying that the worms were too deeply imbedded in the flesh. Still, none came out. But the lye ate away at the skin, and now my legs are all bound up with oil-drenched linen. It heals very slowly, and I have a hard time walking.

Here everybody is greatly surprised: Thresl has consented to marry old Straihamer. The wedding will be next Sunday at St. Anne's. This means that two big bundles of money will now come into one bag. I would never have thought that she would come around.

I hope your spinet has safely arrived. Maybe your husband will be good enough to hire you a music master. You played quite well; it would be a pity if you lost your skill. (Signor Pasquali still cannot get over it that you are not his pupil anymore; you were the most diligent one he ever had, he says.) The other day I tried to play the little saraband you always liked so much, but my fingers are all swollen and stiff.

Keep yourself in good health, and let me know right away if I may hope for a grandchild.

Your devoted mother,
Brigitta Cammerloherin, Widow

◈

JACOB SCHRETTER, IN VIENNA, TO MONSIGNOR MICHAEL KIRNSPERGER, DEACON OF ST. MARY'S IN INNSBRUCK

This 25 Aprilis, Anno Salutis Nostrae 1683

Amice Carissime:
God has given us great joy: My wife is with child. She is of good cheer, save that she gets very sick in the morning and cannot keep food down at that time of the day. May God give her an easy time of it. I do hope that she is not bemoaning her fate by now, for I doubt, dear friend, whether Barbara would have consented so readily to marry me, a man twice her age, had the late Cammerloher (whom we both knew as Christendom's epitome of petty tyranny) not played unwittingly into my hands by refusing to let her drive to the Aigen Fair. And *that* at the last moment, when the horse was being hitched to the carriage. He needed the carriage, he suddenly announced. I happened to be calling at the Cammerloher house just then, and feeling an urge to spite the old quill-driver (Old! — he was my senior by a mere moon), I offered to take Barbara and her friends to the fair in my carriage. After a day of downright Saturnalia (my desire for gingerbread, apple cider, and target shooting has

been met for the next thirty years), I brought Barbara home. As we arrived at the Swan House, she appeared almost reluctant to enter. Had I been twenty years younger, I would have asked Cammerloher for his daughter's hand then and there. Yet reason prevailed. I left Salzburg the next day. Three weeks later, after due reflection, I felt certain that I wanted Barbara to be my wife and, God willing, the mother of my children. So I presented my demand and was accepted by the worthy Cammerloher. Barbara still seemed quite eager to leave the parental home. I do hope she did not buy herself a lentil dish—she is somewhat restless as of late—perhaps this will cease when she has the child.

We will be going out to the garden in this fair weather, only I will have to pay great attention to restrain Vitus from driving too fast. We will take the longer road so as to avoid passing by Gallows Hill, and I will have Vitus and Margaret clean the garden of toads, snakes, spiders, and the like which could frighten Barbara into miscarrying (which God forbid).

Leopold Kohlröser came to see us on furlough from his garrison in Eisenstadt. He was greatly disturbed when we told him the news of his sister's marrying the old quack. (My wife's mother related this to us in a letter. Sapienti sat.)

Wishing you a Blessed Easter Time, I send you my heartfelt greetings.

Your devoted friend,
Jacobus Schretter

BARBARA SCHRETTER, IN VIENNA, TO HER MOTHER, BRIGITTA
WIDOW CAMMERLOHER, IN SALZBURG

St. Pancratius Day, in the Year of the Lord 1683

My Dear Mother:

You shall be pleased, I trust, by what I have to tell you. I am with child.

I am happy and feeling good, save that I am quite ill in the morning. Margaret makes me eat dry bread and drink warm wine, but I am having a hard time keeping it down.

We were disturbed by your news about Thresl. I wrote to her, yet did not get any answer. Have you seen her these last few days?

The flowers have come out in the warm sun, but also the fleas and bedbugs. Margaret says this is a particular flea year. Jacob had the ground floor laid with new bricks. You should have seen the fleas jumping out when the carpenters ripped off the old boards. Margaret and Cathrin scrubbed all the floors and strew bay leaves everywhere. It smells good. We also shook out all our clothes and furs and hung them out in the sun. One picks up the vermin so easily with the skirts.

Then we went after the bedbugs. They hatch so fast that last week I felt as if I were lying on an anthill. We have taken all the bedsteads apart and smeared a salve of goosefat and caraway seeds into every crack. It helped—now we are bitten only once or twice a night.

The flies plague us very much, not only houseflies but also horseflies that come in from the street. Cathrin hung a wolf's tail on the wall, for it is said that flies cannot stand the sight of a wolf's tail, but they were still buzzing around. Xaver said it was probably a dog's tail, since the flies did not care.

Last Sunday it was hot in church and lots of flies were buzzing around. Pater Anselmus was annoyed and preached against them, saying that the Devil sometimes takes on the shape of a big fly-swarm, as happened last year in Znaym. In this guise, Pater Anselmus said, the Devil works all kinds of strange business; thus Christ called him the "Lord of the Flies." On the way home Jacob said that he had seldom heard a sillier story, for if the Devil wanted to show himself, it would rather be in some fair shape, the way he did when he was tempting St. Anthony. Jacob also said that the Devil would hardly choose a church during Mass to show himself and that Pater Anselmus was a ninny.

We are also overrun with mice. Balthazar, Jacob's tom, is of no help at all—he only goes for walks on the roofs, comes home all scratched, and needs to be fed. Margaret said one should cut off his ears, for this would make him a good mouser, and my husband told her that he would cut off *her* ears if she wanted to cripple one of God's creatures just for her own convenience. Margaret laughed and said that Jacob had a weak constitution which fears blood. She is still angry at him because a fortnight ago the miller from Hadersdorf was beheaded in the High Market Square and she had gone to watch. When she came home she brought with her a pint bottle full of blood. She had bargained with the hangman for it, for many apothecaries say that blood from a beheaded man has great healing power and she wanted to use it in a salve against Jacob's gout. But when he saw the bottle he got angrier than I have ever seen him. He called it an unholy, un-Christian superstition and told her to take the bottle with the blood and bury it in the yard right away. He followed her and made us all come into the yard. When the bottle was covered with earth he said a Pater Noster over it and asked God for mercy on the poor sinner's soul. Afterward Margaret said he could keep his gout —she would never again move a finger for him. It made me angry and for a while I did not speak to her.

Tonight we will have guests: Cavaliere Ricasoli, his son, and Ambassador Magalotti. We have hired Jeannot (here they call him Schani), the Duke of Rohan's second cook, and we will serve:

> Crabs in basil
> Salad with olives
>   (they sell olives in the apotheca)
> Roast duck
> Green bass
> Cucumber salad
> Egg cheese
> Apples in honey
> Coffee and Benedictine

I wondered whether this was not too modest a fare for those gentlemen, but Jacob said no, the Florentines were not as greedy as the Viennese. When they get together, instead of only stuffing themselves like pigs, they want also cheerful talk and good wine.

Jacob will bring up a few bottles of '79 Tokayer from the cellar. I will wear the dark brown silk dress with the Brussels lace. It still fits me.

I kiss your hands. May God bless and keep you.

Your obedient and loving daughter,
Barbara

*FROM THE COOKBOOK OF JEANNOT, SECOND COOK TO
THE DUKE OF ROHAN*

Green Bass

*Take the bass, cut it into pieces, and wash the pieces. Put
them on skewers and roast them evenly. Salt them to
taste. Take raisins, let them soak in wine, add half a
lemon. Cook the wine with the raisins and lemons, add
cloves, pour this sauce over the roasted fish pieces. Serve
forthwith.*

BARBARA SCHRETTER, IN VIENNA, TO THERESIA KOHLRÖSER,
IN SALZBURG

St. Pancratius Day, A.D. 1683

Dearest Thresl:

My mother writes to me that you have consented to marry
old Straihamer. Is this the truth? Pray write to me right away
and put my mind at rest.

I am with child. Jacob is very pleased, and my mother will
be happy. I hope I will keep all my teeth, although they say
one child—one tooth. My mother has only nine left.

Write to me, I pray you.

Your loving friend,
Barbara

As the Taxis Mail does not go until day after tomorrow, I re-open this letter to tell you about a dinner party we had last night. As I wrote to my mother, we expected Cavaliere Rica-soli, his son, and Ambassador Magalotti. We got the Duke of Rohan's second cook for the occasion; he hires himself out all over town on his free days. He came with two of his apprentices and drove Margaret into fits ordering her around like a scullery maid and pinching Cathrin. He came to 50 florins and 10 florins overtime, but it was worth it.

I wore my dark brown silk dress with the Brussels lace and the emerald earrings Jacob gave me when I told him that I was with child. They had belonged to his mother.

At seven the Ambassador's carriage drove through the big entrance door into the courtyard. Jacob received them right at the foot of the staircase and led them up into the library, where he offered them some cordials. Through the door I heard them talk and laugh while I checked the table setting one more time. I had brought out my best damask table cloth, my Dutch plates, crystal glasses, and the silver center-piece with the little statues of Bacchus and Ariana which has been in Jacob's family for over a hundred years. Every-thing seemed in order, so I told Vitus to light the candles. He had hardly finished when Jacob entered with our guests. They greeted me with great ceremony. Ambassador Maga-lotti brought forth a gift for me — a small vial made of rock crystal suspended on a gold chain to wear around my neck. In the vial — he took out the tiny cork — there was essence of orange flowers. The Ambassador said that he was an ex-pert on *all* smells, that to know them is a great and noble science, that each person should have a fragrance to call his or her own, and that the orange flowers seemed to him to have my essence. I was very pleased and wore it forthwith. He then gave Jacob a little leather-bound volume, and Jacob was beside himself with pleasure.

Andrea Ricasoli—this is the young Cavaliere; his father's name is Orazio—presented me with a fan, all of ivory and green silk, you should see it! to carry at my next ball, since it always gets "as hot as Purgatory" there.

Ambassador Magalotti escorted me to the table. At first our guests quite courteously strove to talk German, but soon they began to slip back into their mother tongue and even more so when Andrea said that my Italian is very good (and Jacob speaks it as if he had been born Italian). You can imagine that quite a few things escaped me, for they talked fast and laughed a lot, but I could always make out what they were talking about.

I was a little nervous about whether they would like the fare. As it turned out, they liked it very much, and the Ambassador was pleased that the dishes were not overspiced, for this, he said, dulls and burns your tongue so you cannot appreciate the taste of each dish. Cavaliere Ricasoli said that Redi would approve of the evening's cooking. This man Redi (I will come back to him) always spoke against heavily peppered meat, too many sweets, and too much wine. He said that if people would eat moderately they would neither need nor want the vile medicines ignorant apothecaries are brewing for sick folk and that many a man eats himself to death.

This Redi, Francesco by name, seems to be a great man of letters and much respected in the *Accademia del Cimento* down in Florence. *"Del Cimento?"* I asked. "An Academy of Trouble and Tribulation?"

They laughed at my question and said, indeed, it could be understood that way. Then Jacob explained to me that *"Cimento"* does not mean only trouble or heartache, as in my arias, but first of all, trial, proof. Those men call their Academy *"Del Cimento"* because they want to prove the things they say. They try everything out and do not believe anything from hearsay or because their grandfathers had believed it. Their motto is: *Provando e Riprovando.*

I liked this. As I recall now, I did a little *"cimento"* myself last summer, though unwittingly. My mother had always told me that flowers would wilt if you touch them when you have your monthly time. I happened to have a bunch of daisies in a crock and changed their water, remembering too late that I was having my days. After a while I looked at the flowers again, expecting them to be all dried up. Yet they were as fresh and pretty as before. I did not think much about it at the time, but now I wonder whether I should not put a few more of those sayings to the *cimento*, beginning with Margaret's *Quodlibeticus.*

They also talked about other men at the *Cimento.* Ambassador Magalotti seemed to set great store by his mathematics teacher, whose name I have forgotten, but who had studied with a Signor Galileo, who got in trouble with the Jesuit Fathers for saying that the sun does not move around the earth, but that, on the contrary, the earth moves around the sun. I said I did not understand why they had such a squabble over this, for it might just have been that Signor Galileo's eyes were tricked, as happens to me when I ride in the carriage and Xaver drives fast and the roads are dry. At such times it seems as if trees, fields, and houses were flying by and I were sitting in one place. And since—unlike the carriage—we cannot halt either sun or earth, why make ourselves wretched trying to find out whether we sit or move? All we need to know is that God made the sun to shine upon us.

This I said in German because my Italian is not good enough for such a long thought, but Jacob translated it and all three of our guests laughed and applauded me. The Ambassador said that this showed again how all things in life have different meanings, depending on the side from where one looks at them. "For instance," he said, "I laugh when I see one of my peasants blow his nose into his fingers and throw away what came out and I call the peasant a pig. Yet maybe this peasant thinks that I am a far greater pig than he is, for he sees *me* blowing *my* nose daintily, decorously, into a piece of the finest linen bordered with Flemish lace and fragrant with essence of Cordova and then roll the precious product of my nose in this fine handkerchief and keep it on my person. And then a Chinese, when he wants to blow *his* nose, takes out a piece of paper, blows into it, rolls it into a ball, and throws it away. This Chinese, of course, will hold that we both are pigs, the peasant as well as I."

Everybody laughed at this, but they said that Signor Galileo's eyes were not tricked, for he had worked a long time on his spyglasses (some of which are called microscopes), and through them you can see the tiniest creatures crawling around. They said those glasses cost a lot of money; Straihamer must have paid a pretty penny for his. (This reminds me: Pray do not delay, write to me on the spot. I cannot believe that you will marry him, unless—God forbid—there has been some misfortune.)

To come back to the spyglass: Signor Redi, they said, was very pleased when he got one and for many days would look at flies, caterpillars, and maggots on rotten meat.

The gentlemen had such a good time, recalling countless worm and flea stories, and I had to laugh a little because Jacob, who does not even want me to look at a mouse for fear it might upset me and thus endanger the child (which God may prevent), thought nothing of having me listen to those dreadful tales. Perhaps he thought that I did not catch all of it and surely I did not, but I heard a lot of "vermi" and when Ambassador Magalotti began again, ". . . and do you remember when the big tarantula . . . ," Andrea Ricasoli rose to his feet, came over to my chair, and said, "Signora Barbara, one has to have a stomach made of cast iron to listen to this talk. Would you not rather favor me with some music?" "Willingly," I said, partly because in truth I was feeling somewhat sick over Signor Redi's work and mainly because I hoped Andrea would sing again. Therefore we excused ourselves from the three gentlemen who, after giving me their reverence, quickly sat down again to continue their talk. We went over to the spinet, and I played him the Folía and some sarabands and gigues, but not the one from the ball, for I did not want him to know how much I was still thinking of that evening. Then I asked him to sing. He looked through my music books and was pleased to find Begli Occhi there. Remember when you sang it with Poldi? This time I did your part, which was difficult since I had to play as well. Afterward I said I wanted to hear the canzonetta again, the one he sang under my window on Shrove

Tuesday. It sounded so lovely that it lured the gentlemen away from their bugs and worms, for they presently came over to us and asked for more. Andrea knows so many beautiful and gallant airs, and I blessed old Pasquali and his figured bass lessons we always found so tedious, because I could easily keep up with Andrea. The Ambassador said he felt royally entertained at the Casa Schretter, where there was such good cheer, good company, good music, and good wine.

Then we went back to the table, which in the meantime had been cleared for coffee and Benedictine. They talked about many more things of which I heard for the first time. The Ambassador told us of his travels to England and to the Northern Countries—he has even been to Sweden, where the sun does not set in the summer. I was openmouthed that a Christian could go to Sweden and come back alive (I had known about that land only from our grandmothers' tales. As you know, they thought the Swedes worse than the Turks), but no, the Ambassador said, they are quite well-bred, as most people are, he believes, when you come as their guest. He even knows a couple of Turks and has entertained them!!!

He also related that in Sweden they were beset by witches and that many women there were burned and hanged after having told how they were wont to fly through the air and meet the Devil. Now one day a new town judge came, and he ordered some of the women to be bound to their bedposts and to be watched. The women fell asleep. But the next morning they still told about a journey through the air, although they had not left their beds.

Andrea and Cavaliere Ricasoli heartily laughed at this,

but my husband shook his head at this tale and said, "Sometimes I shudder not only at what some folks are, but even more, at what they think they are."

It was almost one o'clock when they took their leave. They said they had enjoyed the evening no end. The Ambassador invited us to his residence for next week; he will send a courier around to ask which day would be convenient. I thanked them, curtsied, and retired. Jacob escorted them to their carriage. I still could hear them laugh in the courtyard. Then the carriage door banged shut and they clattered away.

Jacob came back into the house and said it had been a delightful dinner and he was proud of me — what a gracious hostess I had been to his friends. Then, half in jest, he kissed my hand and said he was going to bed and to join him soon. But I did not want to go to sleep before I had put down what I remembered from Andrea's serenade, so I went back to the spinet, found some music paper, pen, and ink. Replaying what I had retained from it, I wrote down as much as I could. And so intent was I on my task that I was still writing when the candles flickered out and I saw that the morning light was coming through the shutters.

Here you are — ten pages written since last night, not counting the music. My fingers are as stiff as sticks.

Dearest Thresl, write to me.

Your loving and concerned friend,
Barbara

I have now a new music master, Signor Poglietti. He is Imperial Organ Master and gets 3 florins a lesson.

FROM BARBARA'S MUSIC BOOK

Barbara's Hand

Begli Occhi, non trovo	Warm glances, no maiming
Fierezza e dolore.	Through pride or through sorrow
I pianti non trovo	I feel by your aiming
Nel regno d'Amore.	Of blind Cupid's arrow.
Qual or mi mirate	Ah, now in your gazing
Con sguardi amorosi	It's joy that you're after
Scherzate vezzosi.	Your eyes are all laughter.

Voi labbra ridenti	Such laughter once heard, how
Quest' alma beate	My spirit rejoices!
Sì cari gli accenti	I drink every word, O
Sì dolci formate.	What sweetness your voice is!
Se i denti scoprite	And when your teeth glisten
Con rare bellezze	A dazzle of whiteness
Nutrite dolcezze.	I feed on that brightness.

Andrea's Hand

Ma, lasso, pavento	But winds could be nearing
Che un ciel bello e puro	Those skies warm'd by sunlight,
Al soffio d'un vento	And clouds then appearing
Sì cangi in oscuro.	Would bring on cold midnight.
Quell' auro che spira	Pure air now surrounding
Quel guardo che alletta	These glances that fill me
S'adira e saetta.	Could blacken and kill me.

MONSIGNOR MICHAEL KIRNSPERGER, DEACON OF ST. MARY'S IN
INNSBRUCK, TO JACOB SCHRETTER, IN VIENNA

Idibus Maii, Anno Salutis Nostrae 1683

Amice Dilecte,

This, indeed, is welcome news. Give my good wishes to
your spouse and tell her in my name to keep herself in good
health.

You hope for a son—what a wondrous thing it is that a
father always likes it better to have begotten a son than a
daughter. Maybe it is because he wants his lineage to continue or because sons are stronger than daughters. "Thesaurus vanus est filia patri suo," says Ben Syrach, the wise
Jew, in his Proverbs. Syrach also says, "Whosoever has many
women around him also has many an opportunity to further sorcery"—but this, I think, is slandering the honest
and honorable female sex. However that may be, one should
welcome what God sends, be it son or daughter.

Children are God's blessing. When one sets out to raise
children, one should give great attention to them. Keep
them from pettiness, stubbornness, fear, sadness, and other
troubles. Give them what they need, and defend them from
hurt. Keep them well in body and soul. The soul of a child
is like a clean slate on which nothing has yet been written—you can write on it whatever you want. Should you
have an ill-tempered child of bad behavior, begin to guide it
toward a good disposition, step by step, with gentleness and
punishment. Yet one should never punish a child too
harshly, for this does not work. Only when it is not too se-
vere can punishment be recommended. Gentleness is at its

best when it is paired with order. Sometimes it is advisable to overlook a little mischief if by forgiving it a greater evil can be avoided.

However, it is a little hasty to make all those recommendations. For the time being, let us pray for a safe and happy delivery of your dear wife.

The new church is almost finished. His Eminence wants me to move into the new Presbyterium right away, which I do not want to do. I cannot commend all this recent madness for building; such stone heaps do not profit anyone. Romulus and Remus grew up in a shepherd's hut, Caesar in a little house. Cato did not want to live in a palace, and Diogenes dwelt in a barrel. We had a narrow abode in our mother's womb, and in a narrow place will we lie when our time is over. So why do we want so much room while we live?

God's blessing to you and your wife.

As for the lentil dish, pray do not worry yourself and be of good cheer. I credit your wife with having more sense than that; moreover, she will have a family soon and thus no time for fancies.

Salve atque vale.

Your devoted friend,
Michael Kirnsperger

BRIGITTA CAMMERLOHER, WIDOW, IN SALZBURG, TO HER
DAUGHTER, BARBARA SCHRETTER, IN VIENNA

This May 25, in the Year of Our Lord 1683

Dear Daughter:

I thank God for the welcome news and pray that He may keep His hand over you.

Take good care of yourself. Do not stretch; do not carry anything heavy. Sometimes it happens that in the third month a woman wants to eat all kinds of untoward things, such as eggshells, chalk, glue, wheel grease, live fish, and the like. Should you feel such cravings, you may be sure that you are carrying a girl. If you have a desire for rabbit meat, you might get a child with a cleft palate (which God may prevent).

Do not disturb yourself over Thresl. I trust you will hear from her in due time.

Your husband, I fear, is something of a miscreant, and I wish he would not say such things aloud (as regards the Devil) for one never knows who might be listening. For your sake, if not for his, he should be more careful.

Write to me soon and tell me all about your dinner party. I hope you watched your larder while this Schani was at work in your kitchen. I do not care *whose* second cook he is; never trust any of those day-by-day servants.

As for entertaining a group of men, there is nothing easier than that for a woman. All she needs to do is to serve good food and to keep her mouth shut. The men will do the talking and the more you let them do it, the louder they will praise you as a truly excellent hostess.

Your loving mother,
Brigitta Cammerloher, Widow

*FROM BRIGITTA CAMMERLOHER'S COOKBOOK, NOW
OWNED BY BARBARA SCHRETTER*

Poppy Soup

*Put two handfuls of poppy seeds into your pepper mill
and grind them fine. Pour a pint of water over them and
let them stand overnight. Force them through a piece of
linen and save the water. Put the poppy seeds and the
water into a pot. Add a clump of butter the size of a wal-
nut, three cuts of white bread, a handful of ground al-
monds, a spoonful of honey. Salt to taste. If the broth gets
too thick, add a little water. Bring to a boil, remove
quickly from the fire and serve. These soups are good
against sleeplessness.*

BRIGITTA CAMMERLOHER, WIDOW, IN SALZBURG, TO HER
SON-IN-LAW, JACOB SCHRETTER, IN VIENNA

This June 6, A.D. 1683

Dear Son-in-Law:

I beseech you earnestly to burn this letter as soon as you
have read it, lest perchance your wife might find it and
come to grief over it (which God forbid) since she is with
child.

She has written to the Kohlröser girl, she tells me, and
wonders why she does not receive any answers. Pray find
some excuse should she speak of her puzzlement to you, for
the truth should not be told her right now.

I shall relate the events as faithfully as I can.

Last month we had the pox here in Salzburg. Many chil-

dren were stricken; not a few of them died. When little
Elias died, the youngest of the Schultzin's who lives near St.
Anne's Gate, the Schultzin said she was certain that old
Emerentz (you saw her once, she sometimes washed and
scrubbed for me) was spreading the pox among the children
and that Emerentz was a witch who needed the bodies of
the innocent for her sorceries. The Schultzin once saw
Emerentz in St. Peter's cemetery, going 'round and 'round
the fresh grave of a child, and went to the Alderman with
her tale. The Alderman sent out the Town Guards to get old
Emerentz. They searched her garret, but did not find any of
the things necessary for witchery. So they merely put her in
the Castle dungeon until such time as they could bring her
before the Judge. Four weeks later she was brought before
Judge Perckmayr, a very learned man. There were many
folks in Court that day. I also went because we all knew
Emerentz and the Schultzin. Judge Perckmayr asked the
Schultzin to repeat her complaint. When she had done so,
he asked her how she explained that children, men, and
women were still dying from the pox while Emerentz, who
had been kept in the dungeon, surely could not have gone
around spreading the sickness. The Schultzin answered that
Emerentz had been doing it through the walls with the help
of the Devil. At this the Judge waxed angry indeed and said,
"And do you not think that if she had the power and the
Devil's help to spread the pox, she would have, first of all,
brought them on you? But I see that you are hale and
healthy."

Then he said that though he knew about the evil forces of
sorcery he would not abide those overeager folks who, every

time there is a sickness or any other woe, are quick to cry: "Witch, witch." Yet everybody knows, the Judge said, that many evils are caused by the influence of comets. With that he made the Schultzin pay a fine of 50 florins for having sinned against the Eighth Commandment and set old Emerentz free. This would have been all, but it so happened that when they brought Emerentz home, the Captain of the Guards, who is the Schultzin's brother, went through the garret again. He looked into every nook and cranny and at last, hidden under an old straw mattress, he found three stockings full of gold coins. They brought her back into Court.

The Judge was now rather angry at her because he thought she might have done some witchery after all. He questioned her for quite a while, but could not get anything out of her. So he had her put on the rack. There she confessed that over the years she had received the money from women whom she had helped to free themselves from shameful childbirth. She gave about half a dozen names and one of them was that of the Kohlröser girl.

The next day they came for Thresl. When he saw the Provost entering his house and putting irons around the girl's wrists old Kohlröser suffered a stroke.

They brought her into Court, along with four other women. At first they denied everything, but then the Judge threatened them with the Slipper. This made them admit having bought several draughts from Emerentz to rid them of their shame.

The Judge took pity on the girls. He said there were no grounds for hanging them since they had not killed anybody, a child in the womb having no soul for the first three months. Thus the girls were merely to be flogged 25 lashes each, their hair was to be cropped, and they had to pay a fine of 50 florins each. He also said that he would not have them flogged in the Market Square as the whipping of half-naked young wenches would only cause lewdness in the bystanders, who already were a sinful lot. If they wanted something for their edification, he said, he was willing to have Emerentz whipped for them in the square. This caused much grumbling, and some said the Judge should be careful lest he be accused of abetting sorcery. For five months no one had been hanged or burned for witchcraft in this Town. But those who talk that way may still have to wait awhile, for the Judge is a friend of the Archbishop and dines with him at least once a week.

The next day Thresl and the four other girls were whipped in the courtyard of the Fortress. Their hair was cut off. They say that afterward the Provost sold Thresl's hair for 70 florins to a wigmaker, who said that his lady customers always want blonde wigs.

After Angelus the Judge had them loaded on a cart and dumped at the doorstep of their houses. All the other girls were chased away, their families not wanting them anymore, but the Kohlröserin made Thresl enter by the back door and helped her up the stairs into her room. Thresl fell forward on the bed. Her back was covered with bleeding welts and her shirt was stuck to them. We had to pull it off, causing her great pain. We tried to get some food into her, but she could not keep anything down. By midnight she had a fever. The Kohlröserin had to go downstairs to see after her man, who died at dawn. God rest his soul. I stayed upstairs with Thresl while they held the wake. As soon as Kohlröser was buried I went home.

Last Sunday night I heard someone knocking at the entrance door. I had to go and open myself, for old Rosalia thought it was a dying soul announcing its passing and could not budge for fright. I looked through the peephole, and there stood Thresl, dressed in servants' clothes, a kerchief 'round her head, and a bundle in her hand. I led her into the kitchen and made her sit down. She said she was leaving home while her mother was asleep for she could not bear the shame she had brought upon her parents. She thanked me for what I had done for her (it was little enough) and at last told me that it had been Count Kuenburg, the Archbishop's nephew, who had brought her to disgrace. It happened after the sleigh ride and the Wirtschaft at the Castle on Rose Monday. She had had one glass of Tokayer too many and could hardly recall how it had come about. (I thank God that I never allowed my daughter to attend those merriments, as many a girl afterward had reason to be sorry that she went.)

When she first felt that she was with child she went to Emerentz—other girls had talked to her about the old woman's medicines—and bought some senna juice from her. But this merely made her ill. When she returned for another recipe she came just in time to see Emerentz taken away by the Town Guards. She took fright and went to Pater Crispin for confession. He told her that she was fortunate indeed that Dr. Straihamer wanted to marry her. To spare her family and herself great shame she should consent to marry the doctor right away, this being the cross she should bear in atonement for her sin. But when Emerentz confessed

on the rack having sold the senna juice to the girls everything came out into the open. Thresl said she was glad, after
all; she rather would live in shame and poverty than with
the old quack. She also said she was glad that her brother
was down in Hungary fighting the Turk, for had he been in
Salzburg he surely would have tried to kill the Count and
would have ended on the gallows.

Then she embraced me and thanked me again. In return,
I said, she must promise me on the Cross not to try to do
away with her child should God allow her to carry it to
term. This she did. I gave her a basket with some food and
an old coat of Barbara's, and she went away. A few days
later Emerentz was found hanged in her garret. She had
been out of her mind ever since they had released her after
the whipping. She fancied that she saw the hangman everywhere, and that he was trying to put her on the rack again.
Judge Perckmayr was much blamed for this; folks said if he
had had old Emerentz hanged she could have saved her soul
beforehand, but now that she has killed herself she has died
in sin and will be damned and it is the Judge's fault.

Straihamer has brought a lawsuit against the Kohlröserin
because, he said, she had led him to believe that her daughter was a virgin when he asked for her hand.

This is what happened.

Take good care of Barbara. I wish you health and happiness. I also wish you would not jest in the open about
matters of religion, for sometimes the walls have ears.

God be with you and your wife.

> Your devoted mother-in-law,
> Brigitta Widow Cammerloher

JACOB SCHRETTER, IN VIENNA, TO MONSIGNOR MICHAEL
KIRNSPERGER, IN INNSBRUCK

This July 3, A.D. 1683

My Dear and Learned Friend:
This might well be the last letter I will ever write to you in
this life (absit omen). I entrust it to my dear wife, as I entrust her to your protection. I do not think that I am pre-
suming too much on your friendship in sending Barbara to
Innsbruck; my reasons are weighty and cogent.

It is clear to everyone save the Emperor that the Turks
will be at our walls within weeks, nay, days. Poldl Kohlröser,
on his last visit here, told me that his regiment (Caprara's)
was to be billeted in Pressburg, a sign that our chiefs and
captains are reckoning with a siege. His Majesty, however,
goes blithely about his usual business, i.e., opera and the
hunt.

Yet I would wager my last farthing that he would leave
this instant if he understood what Starhemberg, Caprara,
and Cappliers have taken upon themselves to tell him,
namely, that the Turks are coming. I admit to you, dear
friend, that my thoughts were not so unlike those I am lend-
ing to the Emperor (absit laesio Maiestatis), especially since
Barbara is with child. But yesterday I learned that Count
Kollonitsch (who was made Bishop of Neustadt not long
ago) had decided to remain in the city along with Liebenberg and Grüner, the Rector Magnificus. They said that,
even if the Ruler should take to flight, at least some of his
trustworthy servants must stay with the townsfolk in times
of calamity and see to it that authority be maintained and

the enemy met in due battle order, by the citizens as well as by the soldatesca.

I was ashamed of my cravenness and announced that I, too, would stay, at which they were much pleased.

As my wife would be of no help, but rather unnecessarily exposed to danger, I am sending her forthwith to Innsbruck while the city gates are still open. Pray find her suitable quarters. She is traveling with old Margaret, the servant girl Cathrin, and two coachmen. She is provided with sufficient money for all her expenses. Furthermore, I am enclosing a letter of credit drawn on the House of Feroni in Innsbruck, should she be in need of funds.

Dear friend, I do not know how to thank you for this. If God wills me to die, we will meet again in a better world where, at last free of my gout, I will take a walk with you through the Garden of Paradise.

However, if He allows me to live, then, dear friend, I will look forward to a dinner of roasted pigeons in your company, where I will relate our vanquished troubles to no less distinguished an audience than that of the late Aeneas, when he recited the tale of his travels to Dido and the open-mouthed Carthaginians. Et haec meminisse iuvabit.

May God keep you in good health.

Your grateful friend,
Jacob Schretter

JACOB SCHRETTER'S HAND

This July 6, A.D. 1683

Barbara, my dear Wife:

Will I ever see you again? In this hour of faintheartedness I hardly dare believe it. Whatever came over me to covet the post of Town Councilor? I may have taken too much on myself. Still, whosoever says A also must say B. God willing, and as long as He lends me life, I shall do my best to help see the townsfolk through this time of trouble. The Bishop wants me to keep a record of our tribulations, so I begin this diary in nomine Domini.

July 7

The Emperor has left town. However, one hour before he set out for Korneuburg he received a delegation from the Town Council. He promised them that he would see to it that help would be forthcoming, hora certa, incerta quando. Much obliged. Then he turned tail, not before permitting the members of the delegation to kiss his hand.

Starhemberg is appointed Commander-in-Chief. The city gates are now shut and barricaded. God help us all.

July 10

No time for the diary during the last three days. I can hardly hold the quill—witness my handwriting—as my fingers are stiff and swollen from shoveling at the walls. The bastions are crumbling.

Announcement with drums: Every house must have at least ten buckets of water under its roof.

Item: Five hundred men to report immediately to work on the walls. I have the sad satisfaction of seeing my past warnings and misgivings justified. Everybody is toiling—the Mayor, the Rector of the University, along with tradespeople, beggars, housewives, whores. Hocke is sitting on a boulder, a notebook on his knees, counting men and women, shovels, and wheelbarrows, and making lists of foodstuffs. I teased him a little, saying that he found a way of shirking his duty. He waxed rather indignant, announcing that he intends to write the chronicle of the siege for posterity's benefit. This pleased me indeed, for it absolves me from striving to be the Thucydides of this calamity. Let posterity consult Master Hocke—I for my part will set down whatever comes to my mind, things I would have liked to tell you in good time, perhaps in long winter nights when tales come easily, things I would have been pleased to relate to my son (if God grants us one). Yet fugit irreparabile tempus. So you will find trifles and weighty matters together here, as a man writes them down who has no time to select or prune his words. I pray that this record, this letter to you and our child, will some day come into your hands. Meanwhile let us be of good cheer in our trials.

July 12

Work on the walls. The cannons are placed at last. Bedding the pieces took hours on end—would God those Tartars could be sidetracked by the prospect of some loot in the suburbs—but the suburbs went up in flames two days ago.

Companies are forming and drilling—the Guilds, the students of the University. Almost the whole Faculty has

64

stayed in town, even old Grüner, the Rector Magnificus. They are now working on the walls. Yesterday Kirchstetter, iuris utriusque doctor, was knocked senseless by the recoil of a culverin he had fired in his zeal. He has taken up shoveling again.

Pater Quilici, S.J., is working beside me, together with a few of his colleagues. Serves him right. It was at their advice that the Emperor showed himself so intractable to the Hungarian Protestants that he drove them to align themselves with the Turk. Had we had the help of the Hungarians, the heathens would not be at our walls today. Si cum Jesuitis, non cum Jesu itis . . . .

July 13

Last night the dark sky suddenly brightened with a red glow—Starhemberg has ordered the remaining suburbs to be burned. The Turkish Cavalry has reached St. Marx's. The big woodstack in front of the counterscarp caught fire. We formed a bucket chain, and, with God's help, we were able to quench the flames in the nick of time before they reached the Powder House. As the stack burned, that fool, Baron Zwiefel, fired his pistol into the flames. The bystanders believed this to be some sort of sorcery to turn the flames toward the Powder House (all the more as the Baron had been seen with a couple of Hungarians not long ago). They grabbed and killed him outright, dragged the body to the Armory, and flayed it. He was indeed lucky to be already dead. Starhemberg refuses to punish the ringleaders. He says this very fury could be turned advantageously against veritable spies and renegades, should such be discovered in town.

Mahomet ante portas!

Climbed St. Stephen's tower this morning. If those wretched Turks were not after our skin, one could have truly admired the view from the top; it is worth any of those that Magalotti may have enjoyed while journeying in the East—without the travel fatigue. As I looked down this morning I saw the town surrounded three miles deep by a second town—a city of canvas. I estimated the number of tents at twenty-five thousand—they form a huge crescent around the city. One can easily make out the tent of the Grand Vizier, an affair of green silk shot with silver. You should see it shimmer in the sun! Looked through Starhemberg's spyglass: Soldiers drilling everywhere, hordes of horses, mules, camels. Sappers are preparing their mines. At the city wall our people working feverishly, milling around as on an anthill. I hurried down and manned my shovel again.

The Turks are firing at the Castle Bastion. Luckily the palisades were finished last night, the counterscarp reinforced. Starhemberg was hit by a shell; he has himself carried around on a stretcher.

This afternoon: Long deliberation in the City Council. One must admit it: They all have remained in town; yet I wish some of them had followed the Court. Urgent matters could be dispatched considerably quicker if numerous busybodies did not insist on opening their mouths. Today the question was where to bring the rockets and the ammunition that was stored in the Powder House. It was finally decided to carry all explosives into the burial vaults of the Jesuits, the Dominicans, and the Franciscans. All windows in the crypts will be walled up. Five minutes after the last powder keg was rolled out of the tower, a firebomb fell into the empty vault, but fizzled out, Deo gratias.

Those firebombs, by the way, could use some improvement. Their bark, luckily for us, is worse than their bite. The houses of Vienna, as you know, are built of stone right up to the fourth floor and thus do not burn easily.

A sermon in St. Stephen's. Kollonitsch should forbid those gatherings, and instead should exhort everybody to pray at home or on the bastions. A crowd in times of calamity is ten times worse an explosive than any Turkish mine.

This afternoon a grenade went off in the middle of the church and tore the left foot off old Prisca Hallerin. They bandaged the stump with wine-soaked rags to prevent gangrene. I will go to see her tonight.

BARBARA SCHRETTER, AT ADMONT, TO HER MOTHER, BRIGITTA WIDOW CAMMERLOHER, IN SALZBURG

To Mistress Brigitta Widow Cammerloherin in the House of the Golden Swan, in Salzburg, through the kindness of Monsignor Rauscher

This July 15, A.D. 1683

Dear Mother:

I am writing this in haste, for Monsignor Rauscher will be setting out for Salzburg tonight after Angelus and has consented to take this letter with him.

I know you must have been worrying about me as you must have learned by now that the Turks are before Vienna.

As you can see, I am no longer there, Jacob having sent me to Innsbruck for a safe delivery (if it pleases God) of the child. He himself is staying in Vienna, for he is ashamed that the Emperor has run away. To tell you the truth, I quarreled a little with him, for I wanted to go straight to Salzburg; but he said that Salzburg was looking toward the plain on the north side, wide open to Turkish attacks, should they get past Vienna (which God forbid), while Innsbruck lies safely in the mountains.

I have been on my way these last ten days; Margaret, Cathrin, Xaver, and Vitus are with me. Margaret has heaped the carriage with pillows, so I am not being jolted. We have enough money.

With God's help we will reach Innsbruck in about two weeks. If you would, pray send me a letter to Innsbruck in the care of Monsignor Michael Kirnsperger, Deacon at St. Mary's.

I pray and trust that you are well.

Your loving and obedient daughter,
Barbara

JACOB SCHRETTER'S HAND

July 18

The Leopoldstadt is lost. Those Tartars succeeded in building two bridges over the Danube. After two hours' fighting, Schultz and his cavalry gave up the island.

July 19

The Turks are digging in. They build their trenches incredibly fast, using a great number of Christian slaves. Went up St. Stephen's tower with Starhemberg and looked through his spyglass. You could see those accursed heathens cracking their whips over our people. Should I ever fall into their hands (absit omen) I hope and pray that they will dispatch me quickly.

They are now firing at the Red Tower bastion. The Leopoldstadt is burning like a torch. Starhemberg, unforgivably, had assured the people there that the Imperials would never give up the island. What will become of them? We know all too well.

FROM NICOLAUS HOCKE'S CHRONICLE OF THE
SIEGE OF VIENNA

16 huius

The Worthy Town Council of Vienna has ordered that the womenfolk will fill the dried-up fountains in the squares with water drawn from house wells by means of buckets and that the menfolk (when not employed on the bastions) will quench the fires by means of sprinklers, barrels, and other vessels containing water.

At the order of His Excellency the High Commander, three ad hoc gallows have been speedily made and subsequently erected in three squares, respectively: On the Schottenfreyung, the High, and the New market squares.

17 huius

A call with drums has made known to all and sundry:

All menfolk living in the city who have not yet reported for work on the bastions must present themselves to His Excellency, Count von Daun, to be counted. Whosoever will be found hiding after this call shall be hanged straight under his own window.

JACOB SCHRETTER'S HAND

July 20

Last night they inaugurated the new gallows. A soldier from Dupigny's regiment was hanged. It seems that he had shot his corporal. People are forbidden to gather; yet there was a sizable crowd at the ceremony. Do they never have enough dead and dying to gawk at?

The Law says that bringing a guilty man from life to death should be done in conspectu populi. This is a laudable thought. Punishment, as well as the trial, should be witnessed by all, a warning to the wicked and an edification to the righteous. Yet those wise lawmakers did not consider that a malefactor's dispatching would be nothing more than an amusement for the rabble. No murderer has ever been deterred from a bloody deed, no God-fearing citizen has ever been bettered by watching the last gasps of a wretch on the gallows. It merely makes the good callous and the callous cruel. Here I beseech you, dear Barbara, not to let Margaret take our child to such entertainments, as is the custom of wet nurses and maids. Our child, if God grants us one, will witness death, to be sure, but I want him to see it—for the first time at least—as the moment when the soul goes forth to one of the Three Places and not as a crowd spectacle.

We expect the Turks to storm any day now; therefore all church bells will be silent from now on so we can hear the great one of St. Stephen's. If it rings we all will be on the walls. I have my musket ready.

Dear Barbara, how you would laugh could you see me in such warlike garb. The musket is quite unwieldy—it may well be that I will be shot or run through by one of those fiends before I could even reload the stick, but one shot at least I'll deal them.

I hardly recognize myself. Thin, in less-than-blooming health, I had already chosen a bookish career at an early

age; and look at me now, armed to the teeth and cursing the enemy.

July 21

Night watch at the counterscarp. The summer wind keeps wafting the stench of corpses and dead horses into my nose. Tomorrow we will have to pour quicklime over all of them, man and beast alike.

Hocke is on duty with me. He worries about the quicklime, saying that it could not be done without an express order from the Town Council, mainly because there might be a few persons of standing among the dead who should be buried in their crypts, apart from the soldatesca. He also complained that three days ago he was not relieved from his night watch in time. (Melchior Ruckstätter, the cobbler, who was to take over the watch could not do it for the good reason that he had been blown to pieces by a mine.) Hocke reminds me of your father (to whom God may give a joyous resurrection if such a thing were possible; I fear that on Doomsday Cammerloher will argue questions of protocol or find wrong notes in Gabriel's trumpet). I would like to think that you were better off in my company, gout and all. Est in votis.

BARBARA SCHRETTER, IN INNSBRUCK, TO THERESIA KOHLRÖSER,
IN SALZBURG

At St. Mary's in Innsbruck, This July 22, A.D. 1683

Dearest Thresl:

My mother wrote to me not to worry myself about you and
that I would hear from you in due time. Yet I feel that something is amiss in her words. Whatever it may be, pray tell
me. It could not frighten me as much as do my mother's
soothing words. And write to me at St. Mary's Presbyterium;
the Taxis Mailcoach is taking letters to Salzburg and to Innsbruck.

I am here for my husband has sent me away from the
Turks in Vienna. It was a long journey.

We drove out the Kärntner Gate half an hour before all
the town gates were shut and bolted for good, that is, I rode
with Margaret, Cathrin, and the two coachmen, Xaver—
whom you know—and Vitus. Margaret had heaped the carriage with pillows so I would not be jolted, but after a few
hours of sitting on them I suffered from such a backache
that I threw them onto the carriage floor and sat on the
wooden bench, which, oddly, felt much better.

The southern road was full of folk running away from the
Turks—on foot, on horseback, in carriages. Many beggars
were limping along the carts, asking for alms; there also
were runaway soldiers, even a couple of monks, with everybody pushing and shoving in the heat and the dust. Every
now and then a cart carrying a whole family and heaped
high with pots and pans would topple into the ditch with a
broken wheel, horses would shy, and carriages got stuck in

the dried mud (it had been raining the week before and the sun had baked the wheel tracks).

By Angelus we reached Neustadt. The town was milling with folk from Vienna, the rich filling the inns, the poor camping on doorsteps of churches and houses. We were taken in at the Red Lion. It cost 70 florins and the beds were damp and full of bugs. When I told the host that I was not paying 70 florins to be bitten the whole night, he said that counts and dukes were always staying at his place and none had ever complained.

The next morning we set out early. Xaver left the highway and took to the back roads so we would not be bothered by all those unruly folk. Margaret got angry and said she'd rather be plagued by Christian beggars than killed or dragged into slavery by Tartars (for they were said to roam the woods), but Xaver took us on such hidden by-paths that we saw no one on our way. Those roads, however, shake you all through, and this time I was glad I had my pillows. As I said, we were not troubled, either by Tartars (thank God) or by other travelers; but inns were few and far between. Once we had to spend the night at a farmer's house, and those folks were so wretched that even for money we could get nothing but three cabbage heads, some eggs, and cow-warm milk, all this cooked in a sooty kettle over the fire. The man and the woman let me have their bedstead, but I slept not a wink, for there were not only bugs but also mice in the bed straw. When I paid them with two florins the next morning it turned out that they had never seen such money; only farthings.

We traveled toward Steyr. In a village on the way we

spotted a band of boys dancing around a little heap of logs—they were about to light a bonfire. I wondered why they would want to make a fire at midday in the sun, when I saw that they had a black cat tied to a fencepost amid the logs and were intent on burning the creature alive. I told Xaver to halt and to set the beast free. Margaret was angry with me, but I told her to keep her mouth shut. Xaver, who does not like Margaret, threw the reins to Vitus and jumped off his seat, and I followed him. He pushed the boys aside— they could not have been more than ten years old, a crew of scurvyheads—stomped on the burning logs, drew his knife, and cut the strings that were tying the cat to the post. The poor beast had all its claws out and scratched him, for it was greatly frightened and its tail was already singed. I took it in my arms and ran with it toward the carriage, while the boys threw stones at me and yelled, "Witch, witch!" But Xaver cracked his whip over their heads and we drove off as a few stones hit the sides of the carriage. I drew the leather curtains shut, but Vitus caught a stone on his head.

"That is all we need," said Margaret. Then she said to me, "Indeed, you must have learned such foolishness from the other cat fancier, that husband of yours, and mark my words, he will end up on the gallows or on something worse. That is, if the Turks do not get him sooner."

At this my blood fairly boiled. I threw the carriage door open. "Get out!" I said, and meant it. Xaver who heard me pulled sharply on the reins, and the jolt scared the cat in my arms. He tried to escape (and surely would have been caught again by those wicked boys), so I had to shut the door and told Xaver to drive on.

Margaret glared at me, but kept quiet. She even said nothing when I brought the cat all the way here to Innsbruck; and he is the best mouser you ever saw.

She will not try to kill the cat for she dislikes mice; yet I know that she will seek to get even with me. She never forgets a slight, as you know, but you will not believe this: She does not frighten me much anymore. I think I could get along without her now. She knows it, too.

We continued our journey to Steyr and found lodgings in the Swan. As I made my way upstairs I found myself face to face with Monsignor Rauscher, who had spent the night there on his way to Admont. He was surprised to see me alone, and when I related to him that my husband had stayed in Vienna to be with the townsfolk in their time of trouble, he was most moved and said there was no question of my staying in a wretched inn, but that he would proceed at once with us to Admont and put me up in their guest house.

Thereupon (with much grumbling), Xaver and Vitus harnessed again and the Reverend Father traveled with us to Admont. It was a short journey—only eight hours. The Monsignor was in a great good mood and kept us all laughing, even teased Cathrin, asking her when she would get married and the poor girl blushed (for she most earnestly wants this), but it will be hard for her to catch a man, what with her buck teeth and mousy hair.

At Admont the Prior received me with great kindness. They had news from Vienna: The town was surrounded by the Turks. At dinner, every bite stuck in my throat; I was so greatly worried. And yet it should have been no small pleas-

ure to eat roasted venison from golden plates after having
tasted boiled cabbage.

Monsignor Rauscher set out for Salzburg the next day and
was kind enough to take with him a letter to my mother.
(So you may have known for some days where I am now.)

I rested for two days in Admont and then we set forth toward the Tyrol. We often spent the night in farmhouses
that are clean and whitewashed, not unlike those in our
Salzburg. Once the farmer's folks got very excited, for they
had heard somebody smacking his lips upstairs on the
threshing floor. They said it must have been the Devil, who
likes to sneak up and eat the fresh kernels from the shocks,
and that they perhaps had forgotten to nail two ears of rye
crosswise on the door—this would have kept him away. I
was quite curious to see the Devil eating away at the rye,
but I did not want to offend those good people, although I
thought they were as silly as our Pater Anselmus, who sees
the Devil in every fly.

Nothing much happened during the next few days, until
we came to Rattenberg. As we neared the town gate, we met
a whole crowd of people all hastening toward Gallows Hill.
We passed through the gate into town and halted at the
Blue Ox. The host told us that we came just in time to see
Jörg Wambacher (a poacher and robber) hanged. First they
would pinch him with red-hot irons before stringing him
up. Margaret and Cathrin wanted to go and watch; they
promised to be back as soon as the hanging was done, but I
went upstairs to rest. I do not care to see such things, as you
know. I must have fallen asleep on the spot, for when I woke
up it was late afternoon and Margaret and Cathrin had

come back from Gallows Hill. They told me that the Wambacher certainly had been a handsome man, with a black beard, and Margaret added it was too bad that they did not have the "indulgence" anymore. Neither of us knew what she meant, so she explained to us that many years ago—and even sometimes during her campaign days—a man could be released from hanging if a freeborn woman was ready to marry him on the spot. Cathrin was very much taken by this idea. For several days she would talk about nothing else, moping around, doing no work, only fancying how she would have saved the Wambacher from the gallows.

The next morning we went through Hall and a few hours later arrived here in Innsbruck, where Monsignor Kirnsperger took us in at St. Mary's as my husband had requested of his friend.

In all churches they are praying for Vienna day and night. Many men are enlisting in the Relief Army the Emperor is calling together. Monsignor Kirnsperger finds harsh words for His Majesty, calling him a shepherd who has deserted his flock. He laughed when I related how pale and rickety the Emperor had looked at the Court Ball and said, "Thank God that there are still men in Vienna, such as Starhemberg and your husband. They will show those heathens the way back to Constantinople!"

This made me proud of Jacob and also quite sad. I went up to my room and had to cry for a long while before I fell asleep. When I woke up this morning, I first did not know where I was, for I had slept in so many beds these last weeks. I could hear drums and trumpets from the church square—

new troops were departing for Vienna. We are in great fear —it is said that the Turks are shooting day and night. Not long ago, on the night of the Sleigh Carousel, I had stood with Margaret on the Castle Bastion and she had said that it would crumble under cannonfire like a card house, and she knows about such things from her campaign days. Then what? Would not the Turks storm the Castle? They probably would camp in the Great Hall and shoot at the chandeliers. We will never dance there again. I have not heard from Andrea, or from Ambassador Magalotti, for that matter. There was such confusion in town. Jacob, to be sure, was sad to send me away, but he was somehow quite busy and, indeed, did not pay too much attention to me. I think he wanted me out of the way, and I could swear that he was somewhat excited, gout or not.

Yesterday I felt the child kicking for the first time. God knows what is in store for us.

Dearest Thresl, write to me.

Your loving friend,
Barbara

*FROM THE REPORT OF RUPRECHT STEINSCHNEYDER,
BAILIFF OF THE COLLOREDO FIEF, ARCHBISHOPRIC OF
SALZBURG*

This July 22, A.D. 1683

*Apprehended: Fillgrader, Sebastian, aet. 20, Schön-
bichler, Christoph, aet. 19, for poaching. 3 hares, 4 par-
tridges. 2 hours on the Wooden Horse each, 10 florins
each.*

This July 23, A.D. 1683

*Apprehended: The Woman Kohlröser Theresia, aet. 20,
for truancy.*

*The said woman wore a kerchief around her head.
When seized, declared to be afflicted with scurvy, upon
which she was made to remove said kerchief. This revealed that she had no scurvy at all, but that her hair
had been recently shorn by the Provost. The wench is
with child. Delivered to the Spinning House the following day.*

JACOB SCHRETTER'S HAND

July 22

The enemy has solidly entrenched himself in the Leopoldstadt. This morning three pieces and a rather enormous
mortar are shelling away at the Red Tower. Colalto from
Padua is defending the Red Tower Gate. He lets us fire no
more than two shots at a time. Then he has the cannon
dragged away a few feet before the smoke has cleared and
fired again. It looks indeed as if we had three times as many
pieces as we have.

July 23

A mine exploded a little too soon; about thirty Turks were blown to bits. Arms, legs, beturbaned heads fell on the bastion. This happens seldom, however, the Turkish artillery being otherwise skillful enough, to our chagrin.

BRIGITTA CAMMERLOHER, IN SALZBURG, TO HER DAUGHTER, BARBARA SCHRETTER, IN INNSBRUCK, AT ST. MARY'S PRESBYTERIUM

This July 23, A.D. 1683

Dear Daughter:

I received your letter today. Monsignor Rauscher was good enough to bring it to me as soon as he had put up at the Black Horse in the Linzergasse.

I am glad and I thank God and His Holy Mother that you are safe in Innsbruck, although I would rather have seen you coming straight home.

Your husband says that we could be overrun by the Turks here. God prevent them. I do not believe it yet. The Emperor is getting an army together. At all hours we hear the drums in the streets and alleys. The Arzberger boys have enlisted; so has the late Wannerin's grandson and Burgl Mayr's good-for-nothing man. She might be better off without him.

Quite a few folks from Vienna came here, lock, stock, and barrel, some wealthy, some poor. There are some young men among them who'd look a sight better fighting the heathens than loafing around here. By the same token, your husband, who is not so young and gouty to boot, could have come with you; nobody would have held it against him. I know what he would answer me—namely, that the Mayor and the Bishop are remaining in Vienna though they are even older than he is and that he could not run away from his duties. Yet I say that neither of those two is suffering from gout, nor do they have to think of a family—the Mayor's children are grown and the Bishop would have no business having children anyway.

Take good care of yourself in this heat. Do not drink too much cold beer—it might sour your milk even though you are not halfway through your waiting yet. Eat enough, but not too much, and four weeks before your time comes eat very little, so that the child stays small and can pass easily. Once it is born you can feed it as much as you want and it will gain and grow. But I do not have to write you these things now, for you still have more than five months to go and with God's help I shall be with you when your time is near. At night have Margaret make you a sleeping draught the way I am writing it down for you:

One handful of dried fennel, one spoonful of honey, saffron, and white wine. Let it boil over. This you drink every night before you go to bed. It makes the child strong and handsome. Do not look at snakes, toads, spiders, rabbits, mice, or hunchbacks.

As for myself, my health is as good as I can have it at my age; my left leg is much swollen and one of the veins burst open. They will bleed me tomorrow, but I do not know whether it will help.

Sunday I will go to Maria Plain and say the Rosary for you and the child.

Your loving mother,
Brigitta Widow Cammerloher

I gave the Taxis rider three florins to go to your house as soon as he reaches Innsbruck. If you do the same I might get a letter quickly, in about nine days.

JACOB SCHRETTER'S HAND

July 24

All shingle roofs have been taken down. Seen from St. Stephen's tower the town looks as if one could peer into the very houses from above as did the Devil of the late Señor Guevara. The Topless Towers of Ilion—absit omen.

July 25

Those Turks are the most fanciful of warriors. While their sappers are undermining the town in silence, the Janissars attack to the sounds of hornpipes, tymbals, and bells, accompanied by truly abominable howling. Today we received them as they deserved. A mine threw them up into the air along with a few of our men. Guido Starhemberg, the Commander's cousin, led a sortie and killed a few Turks.

Their heads were stuck on the palisades, presumably to scare the enemy. So far, they merely attract swarms of flies.

July 28

About twenty Turks jumped over the palisades with bared sabers. They got thrown into the ditch and shot there. As I left the bastion today a firebomb fell on the Nuncio's palace. Astonishingly enough, the Town Council's orders were carried out: A bucket chain was formed in no time by women and shopkeepers. If God sees us through this trial Monsignor Galli will have to thank a few ladies of easy virtue for protecting his palazzo and, above all, his library.

August 1

The Turks have drawn so close by now that we could talk to them if we so desired. Instead, we greeted them with grenades and morning stars and they retreated. I was glad I had only a halberd—I can see myself attacking a Turk with such a weapon, but to wield a morning star is beyond my means.

They continue to dig their subterranean tunnels, fortifying them with wooden beams and protecting them with sandbags. There will be fierce fighting should the Turks succeed in emerging in the middle of the town. I wonder how much the fencing lessons at the Jesuit College will profit me then.

Those fencing lessons, Barbara, were the bane of my school days. I circumvented them whenever I could. Our Swordmaster was a scar-covered old corporal from Montecucculi's regiment. He would brag to us at the drop of a hat that he had been a friend of Deveroux and had been present at the dispatching of Wallenstein. The exercises were strenuous and—to me, at least—tedious.

"Faster! Faster!" the corporal would yell. "In a duel you'd already be a dead man!" To shorten those weekly harassments I saved my pocket money—my father providing me but sparingly with funds—to buy flasks of a certain Falerno wine to which my tormentor was partial. Thus mellowed and egged on by me, the old cutthroat would favor me with tales of his exploits until the bell would announce the end of the fencing lesson and I could go back to my beloved Vergil.

I probably will have to pay for this now, should the Turks break through the bastion. Besides, how do you parry a scimitar? God help us all.

August 2

Another sortie, this time by Colalto. Our prisoners: one Turkish officer, two soldiers, and two camels. The townsfolk, though weary and worried, kept staring at the beasts, and truly, they must look queer enough to anyone who has not seen them before. A few lads tried to mount those "ships of the desert," as the Turks call them, but, not knowing how to ride them, the boys were thrown and one so severely that he broke his neck and died on the spot.

August 6

The Turks are throwing sand, dirt, and woolen sacks into the ditch. Several mines exploded at the counterscarp, blowing a dozen of our men into the air. Three of them fell right back on the spot where they had been before. They were unhurt, save that they complained of thirst.

85

One does not have to fly through the air to get thirsty here. Water is getting scarce; many fountains are dry. The house wells have foul water which must be boiled before anyone can drink it. No wonder—from the day the gates were locked and barricaded, no refuse could be brought outside and burned there as was the custom. Dead horses and offal are rotting away in the streets. The heat makes it worse—never have I seen so many flies around. Yesterday I picked several lice out of my hair, which brought me to wash my head with my ration of wine. It did not help much.

August 7

Last night thunderstorms and a heavy rain kept us as well as the enemy from firing our pieces. We let ourselves be soaked to the skin. It was wondrously cool.

August 8

On duty on the Löwel Bastion. In addition to the Turks the flies plague us considerably. The Turks do not promptly remove their dead from the counterscarp, and we certainly cannot risk any of our men to accommodate our noses. Haller is relieving me at the culverin—he is a far better shot than I am. We have been peppering the Turkish trenches for the last two hours—to little avail.

Right now I am sitting on the bare ground, my back against the stone of the inner bastion. A flask is going 'round, but I do not like to drink wine against the thirst. The Souchy officers, however, were less dainty yesterday. They have emptied the Rohan cellar to the last bottle of Tokayer, which greatly annoyed the old Duchess, who had put her palace at the disposal of Souchy and his staff. (She had stayed in town, stating that it would take more than a bunch of Turks to make her budge even an inch.) Now she complained to Kollonitsch about Souchy's ungratefulness, and he listened patiently, though he has, by God, weightier worries. Had she come to me, I would have told her the story of The Herring and the Onions and sent her on her way.

That story, by the way, is a worthwhile tale and contains a lesson. I am writing it down for you:

Once upon a time there lived in Amsterdam a rich ship-owner. One morning he was walking along the Grachten, those narrow lanes bordering the canals (for Amsterdam somewhat resembles Venice), when he spotted an old sailor sitting on a pile of ropes. The rich man was in a good mood—one of his ships had just come in from East India—so he fell to talking with the old man. It turned out that the latter had sailed on the Mynheer's vessels for many years. The shipowner, pleased, invited the sailor to have breakfast in his house on the Gracht. The latter accepted and the two men walked over to the Mynheer's house. They had hardly sat down to a meal of herrings and ale when a servant en-tered the dining room and announced that one of the Myn-heer's friends had come to pay a call. Forthwith the rich man rose, excused himself, and told the cook to take care of the sailor. The new visitor, whom the Mynheer received in his parlor, was another rich shipowner and so it was to be expected that the two began to discuss important business matters. Their talk lasted for two hours, and it was only af-ter his friend had left that the Mynheer remembered his other guest. He went back into the dining room, but the sailor was gone. Gone also were three fine tulip bulbs that had been sitting in a bowl on the window sill. It was clear: The sailor had eaten the bulbs believing that they were onions, without which no fried herring is ever served in Holland. At first the Mynheer was quite angry, but when reason had overcome outrage, he said to himself: "Serves me right. If you invite somebody into your house, then do not leave him to the negligent care of the cook, but give him your best. This poor sailor had expected no less from your hospitality and therefore has rightfully eaten your bulbs. From now on, if you give a man a herring, also give him the onions."

Meanwhile, Haller has used up all the shells and wants me to carry some more up to the piece. It is very hot—we are all in our shirtsleeves.

ANDREA DE' RICASOLI, TRAVELING BACK TO ITALY, TO COUNT LORENZO MAGALOTTI, AT LONCHIO, NEAR FLORENCE

At the Black Swan, Hall, August 11, 1683

Your Excellency, Most Admired and Cherished Friend:
De profundis clamavi, or rather, de altissimis, for I wrote you two letters from Tratzberg Castle where, from my window, I enjoyed a bird's-eye view of the Inn Valley and also the solicitous hospitality of the Khevenhüllers, who send you their heartfelt greetings.

After searching through the trinkets at Innsbruck's jewelry shops I finally found what I think will meet with your approval: to wit, three little perfume flasks made of rock crystal, corresponding to your specifications. The rock crystal is mined by breaking it off from the bare stone high up in the mountains, which accounts for the rather high price of those vials, considering their small size; but I trust the Signora Marchesa will like them, especially because they close hermetically, thanks to the ingenious way the screw-covers are carved. Not a drop of your precious essences will be lost.

Why am I lingering here? You will never guess it. But imagine, last month I happened to stroll under the arcades at Innsbruck where the merchants have their stands. Many women were bustling around, choosing, bargaining, buying. I was idly looking on, for the shape and demeanor of the local viragines are not my style, and, jostled by the crowd, I found myself before a display of silks and linens. The customers fingered the wares with square red hands, but all of a sudden I beheld a white, fine-boned, slightly freckled one with slender fingers that I last had seen running over an ebony keyboard. I could not believe my eyes, which wandered up the sleeve to the shoulder and joyfully recognized the equally freckled, green-eyed countenance of — incredibile dictu — Signora Schretter. Intent on choosing between different kinds of cloth, she did not notice me. I worked my way toward her. "Provando e Riprovando," I said, sotto voce. Ah, you should have seen the scarlet blush running through her cheeks — those redheads have such telltale skin — her hand went to her heart — I was truly flattered. She greeted me with delight. We threaded our way back from the draper's stand — she seemed to have entirely forgotten her errand—and at my question as to what brought her to Innsbruck she related that she was a refugee from the Turkish calamity in Vienna. "I would be enchanted to be your Dioneo," I said, but the line fell flat; she obviously had never heard of Boccaccio. I asked on what day I would be allowed to present my respects to her and to her husband, for I had naturally assumed that Signor Schretter was with her; but she told me (I must admit, with affection and pride) that her husband had stayed behind in Vienna, together with the Mayor, the Bishop, and many of the judges and councilors, to assist the townsfolk in this time of great trouble, as anyone should do who belongs to the authority and even more so in Vienna where, as she put it, the Emperor has run away, "which was a great shame."

Truly I would not have expected such Catonian virtue from our friend Schretter, who seemed rather frail and domestic when I saw him.

She told me that she lived at the new Presbyterium at St. Mary's under the protection of Monsignor Kirnsperger, the Deacon. "Monsignor Kirnsperger is an old friend of my husband," she said, "and, I believe, also of your father." Right then the clock in the Castle Tower struck noon. She excused herself and I accompanied her to her carriage, which was waiting in the Castle Square. There she asked me whether I had ever seen the famous *Black Manikins* in the Court Chapel. "No," I lied, and added, "why not go and look at them right now?" She acquiesced, and we entered the cool, silent church where the statues of twenty-eight mourners—fourteen on each side—stand alongside Emperor Maximilian's sarcophagus. Those statues, cast in bronze, by artists from Innsbruck, represent Kings and Queens of Maximilian's ancestry. They are finely wrought, although our Donatello would have smiled at their stiff countenances; some of them look as if they had just swallowed a dose of castor oil. With childlike amusement Barbara commented on the ladies' garb and the men's heavy armor when I pointed to the statue of Sigismund, Duke of Tyrol. "The artist," I said, "has set an easy task for himself," for Sigismund showed no face. His head was ensconced in a helmet, the visière closed. Was it Sigismund? We had to take the sculptor's word for it.

Barbara smiled but cast an uneasy glance at the forbidding mask. "It scares me," she said. "Who knows what stares at me from behind those eye-slits?" I teased her, saying that as a true honorary Cimentosa she should know that nothing stared, but that Signor Sesselschreib or whatever his unpronounceable name is, simply had used a short cut to finish his duke in time. There is no face underneath, I concluded.

"No face . . ." she said. "That means it could be any face . . ." (Shades of Monsù Pascal!). She shivered a little. We left the church more quickly than we had entered it. I must confess to you, dear friend, that I was relieved when we found ourselves again in the sun-filled square.

As I took leave from her she said, "Why don't you come to dinner tomorrow evening? The Monsignor will be so pleased to welcome you." I accepted with pleasure. The next day, after Angelus, I found myself at table in the new whitewashed refectory of St. Mary's with Barbara (looking ravishing in a modest black silk dress) and the silver-haired

91

Deacon, who turned out to be an accomplished host. However, when it was time to withdraw, he broached a surprise to me, not unlike Jupiter, who let the Titans climb up all the way to Olympus only to hurl them down from greater heights when they fancied that victory was theirs.

I had taken leave from Barbara and Kirnsperger accompanied me to my mount. As I put my foot in the stirrup, he said: "Cavaliere, I have known you since you were three years old. I am a friend of your father. Yet I am also a friend of Jacob Schretter. And I will be damned if I stand by while one friend's son is preparing to put a pair of horns on another friend's head, especially while the latter is absent on an errand of Christian duty. Therefore, Cavaliere, you will do me the favor of leaving Innsbruck tomorrow morning."

He spoke with such good-natured authority that I could not argue with him. So I promised to depart the next day and thanked him again for the delightful evening. "Yes," he said, "it was delightful. Far too delightful. Now go with God, son, and recommend me to your father and to Count Magalotti."

The next morning I packed, had the Signora Marchesa's crystals sent off with a shipment from the Feroni Bank, called for the reckoning at the Golden Eagle, and set out in a carriage for the Brenner Pass and Verona. At three o'clock in the afternoon I halted for some food and wine at a little mountain tavern south of Innsbruck. They had set the table outside on a meadow looking down into the valley. On such luminous summer days the Alps lose their horror sempiternus. Their snow-covered crags appear as though cut out with a gigantic chisel against the bluest sky; woods and meadows are an emerald green cushion cradling, like a jewel, the many-towered Innsbruck. The air, just the right admixture of freshness and sunny warmth, was fragrant with the smell of pine trees and new-cut grass. Peering down I could make out St. Mary's twin bell towers, where I knew Barbara to dwell. Presently I heard someone sing—a sad, rather wailing air. It was a young man who uttered those none-too-cheerful sounds. The innkeeper's daughter joined in. When they had finished their interminable dirge—there must have been at least fifteen verses—I asked them what the words meant. "It is an old tune," the girl said, "and is often sung when someone has to go away. It says:

" 'Innsbruck, ich muss dich lassen.' "

My mind gave a start. "Innsbruck, I now must leave thee?" Who said that I *must?* The old deacon? After all, I had kept my promise. I had left the next morning. I had not promised not to come back . . . I ran to the carriage, pulled off my coatbag, and told my perplexed Vittorio to continue toward Verona. A little later a carter passed with a load of wooden barrels, on his way down to Innsbruck. I climbed up beside him and for half a florin he brought me back down from the Brenner. I deemed it wise not to return to the Golden Eagle, so I transferred my headquarters to the Black Swan in Hall, a borough some ten miles away.

The same evening I proceeded to reconnoiter the territory around St. Anne where Barbara usually goes to Vespers, as she had mentioned the night before in the course of the conversation at dinner. I was lucky—around nine she came out of the cloister, followed by the ubiquitous Margaret. I was standing in the shadow, and as she was about to pass by me I reached out and took her hand. She did not make a sound, was utterly confused, but not altogether surprised. In the meantime Margaret had come up to us and quite unabashedly said to me not to worry, that she was no tattletale and that she would wait for Barbara a few steps ahead.

Far be it from me, dear and venerable friend, to bore you with meticulous descriptions of our many trysts; suffice it to say that for the next two weeks she would come to St. Anne's at night, would hastily distribute her alms, and, instead of attending Vespers, would walk with me along the banks of the Inn. It was easy to obtain her love (indeed, I think I had won her affection already in Vienna), but it turned out to be exceedingly difficult to gain her favors. Amazingly enough, she loved her husband. Sic. Once I was about to say that she had too many scruples, that he only would get what he deserved, leaving his lovely wife for the dubious honor of shooting at Turks (who, by the way, can outshoot any Christian); but I bit my tongue in time for this would have shown me—to her at least—to be afflicted with that "poverty of the heart" which you, dear friend, despise so much.

Margaret abetted those nightly promenades, partly because she was bored and this provided a diversion and partly because she seemed to have a secret little grudge against Schretter and was highly amused by Barbara's uneasy attempts at flightiness.

As for me, I lived only for the evenings. Innsbruck in July can be scorchingly hot; they have a wind there, called the foehn, which is a veritable scirocco, with lots of thunder and lightning, but no rain. It would have been Heaven to run down to the river, throw off all clothes, dive in, and have a good swim; but the natives there are such a bunch of strait-laced bigots, they would have dragged me into Court for shameless behavior (as happened to Gualdi not long ago), and this I could not have, because her Cerberus would surely have been apprised of my arrest and thus of my untimely presence in town.

Last Monday — three days ago — when she came she said that the Monsignore had gone to Brixen and that she had a little more time. We walked over the meadows. There was no moon, but the night sky sparkled, and from time to time a shooting star left a long trail to end behind the mountain. "Lagrime di San Lorenzo," I said. "May I make a wish?" She nodded. I took her hand, leading her to one of the haystacks that stood by the river. And there she gave up all resistance. Afterward I held her in my arms and waited for my heart to calm down. Strangely enough, it did not. She had become mine, I had obtained what I had desired, but, contrary to my other experiences, I loved her more than ever. She was silent and submissive. I brought her back to the church door where Margaret was waiting, kissed her, and pulled a long straw out of her hair. We are to see each other tonight.

Dear and venerable friend, the Signora Marchesa will receive her vials within two weeks, I think. Allow me to kiss her hands.

As for me, may Venus and Mercurius hold their hands over me!

Your admiring and devoted
Andrea de' Ricasoli

◈

JACOB SCHRETTER'S HAND

August 11

Not much shooting tonight. We suspect the Turks are busy with mining. Their engineers know their business indeed; there are half a dozen French renegades (the Plague on them!) among the Turkish sappers. We have put barrels filled with dried peas in many cellars to signal the approach of those deadly moles.

Midnight is tolling from St. Stephen's tower. What a sparkling sky! Every now and then a shooting star traces a wide half-circle across the firmament and falls down on the other side of the Leopoldsberg. At first some of our men believed that they were rockets shot by the Imperials to signal the approaching succor—but this soon turned out to be wishful thinking, for His Majesty, at this hour, is still begging cousins and allies to scrape an army together. I wonder how long we will be able to hold out. No, those fiery sparks—here comes another one—are merely the Lagrime di San Lorenzo, as you know and as we see them every year around this time.

St. Laurentius comes to my mind; not a cheering thought. He was a martyr whom the heathens roasted alive. When King Philip II, the son of Carolus Quintus of glorious memory, besieged and took the town of St. Quentin, the Church of St. Laurentius was destroyed. The King vowed to build the Saint another one and did so in time. The new church and monastery, built in the shape of an iron grate, were consecrated to the Saint. When I was in Spain I visited this church-palace of the King who worshiped the Saint of the fiery death, yet sent thousands to the stake for heresy. And so did Calvin, Philip's enemy, with those who did not share *his* creed. What suffering do we not owe to those absolute spirits. For my part, I hold with Monsieur de Montaigne who wrote that " 'tis to think rather highly of one's opinions to burn a man alive on the strength of them."

In the meantime we have received a couple of shells and a message shot by an arrow. We deciphered it by the light of a torch. It was a call to surrender, written in execrable Latin.

⋖§⋗

ANDREA DE' RICASOLI, TRAVELING BACK TO ITALY, TO COUNT LORENZO MAGALOTTI, AT LONCHIO, NEAR FLORENCE

At the Unicorn in Trent, August 13, 1683

Your Excellency—

Is there truly no greater sorrow than to remember past happiness when you are in misery? I would almost challenge the Divine Poet on this. For as much as I am concerned, I find consolation in thinking of enjoyed bliss, even if it is beyond reach at present. And consolation I need: I am rattled and bruised by an infernal coach that dragged me down here from Hall—I shall continue on horseback as soon as I find a decent mount.

What happened in Hall? It is briefly told:

Barbara did not come that evening, but the next day, around noon, there was a knock at my door. "A lady to speak to you, sir," the servant said. She came in, heavily veiled. I took the veil off her face and kissed her, but she drew away from me and said, "Pray, do not touch me, hear

97

me out, do not touch me, do not make it harder than it is."
And then it came out. She had been to confession. Not to
Kirnsperger, Deo gratias, yet he had noticed her uneasiness
and had asked her whether she had been to communion.
She would have to go to confession first, she said.

At this he sent her to Pater Aegidius at the Franciscans,
for, she said, Kirnsperger thought not much of confessing
one's friends whenever something grave was the matter, and
this he suspected from her mien.

What followed, dear friend, surprised me. I had expected
some zealot to impose fasts and flagellations on her, together
with a fat contribution to the gold encrustation of some local saint's shinbone. Instead, Pater Aegidius turned out to be
a local saint himself (far too much of a saint for my taste).
Here are his exact words, as related by Barbara:

"You are carrying your husband's child," he said. "Thus,
as long as you have no certain knowledge of his death, you
must await in faithfulness the outcome of his lot."

Barbara replied that, even leaving me, she could not call
herself faithful to her husband, as she still would think of
me day and night.

"Evident," said Pater Aegidius. "Let that be your hair-
shirt." And he added, with commendable casuistry, "The
thought alone constitutes no sin. You cannot help it if the
crows fly over your head. But it would be your fault if they
built a nest in your hair." (What a line! Did he pick it up
from Gracián?) Then he absolved her from the sin of adul-
tery and imposed his penance: She was to keep it to herself.
She was never to burden her husband, should he survive,
with a lamenting, selfish confession. And she was not to see
me anymore.

"You will suffer," I said.

"Yes," she replied, "I will suffer. But it will be as with the toothbreaker." I must have looked somewhat puzzled, so she explained: "Whenever you have a bad tooth, it must come out. It hurts, but the wound will heal. Yet if you leave the bad tooth in, then it will suppurate and kill you in the end or at least make you very sick and it will hurt far worse."

I was not too flattered to be compared to a bad tooth and said so. But she merely said, "You understand me. I need the tooth to be pulled out. It will heal in due time and none will be the wiser, unless," she added with a sad little smile, "I open my mouth . . ."

As she seemed indeed determined to leave me, I resorted to the timeworn device of spurned swains—I accused her of not loving me. "I not love you?" she replied. "Oh, Andrea, I lived only for our evenings."

"By the moonclock," I said. Alas, this was ill-advised. Instead of being swayed by this recall of our first encounter, she drew herself together, although with a visible effort.

"Yes, by the moonclock," she said quietly, "and it is all wrong. It shall be the dayclock for me from now on."

She held out her hand.

"Will I ever see you again?" I asked.

"Certainly you will," she answered. "You may come and see me in twenty years, when much water will have flowed down the Inn."

This made me smile, for she obviously saw herself as a wrinkled old crone by that time, while I reflected that she would then be no older than the incomparable Marchesa is today and that I would be just forty-five years old, which indeed would be no age to put aside the things of life and love. Though a long way off, this prospect cheered me a little.

She held out her hand again, but I took her in my arms and kissed her, while tears were running down her cheeks. Then she gently disengaged herself. "I must go now," she said. She walked to the door, holding herself quite straight but moving slowly, as if every step gave her great pain. I dared not follow her.

I departed the same evening, crossed the Brenner and sit now in this wretched inn where they serve old hens and polenta. The place is swarming with drunken carters and pilgrims to Loreto, everybody singing and brawling. The host has announced a curfew after midnight; no one will be allowed to disturb the distinguished guests on the second floor by then. I hope he has informed the bedbugs about this.

I cannot wait to be home again. You are right—it is unreasonable to ask a Florentine to remain for more than six months beyond the reach of the Cupola's shadow.

Dearest friend, Your Excellency, I trust I will find you in good health and spirits at Lonchio. I look forward to long walks with you in the olive groves and to a breakfast of quails, accompanied by a bottle of Montepulciano, near the pond where the fountain splashes down and breaks into a "serenade for five voices" . . .

Pray transmit my homage to the most enchanting and affable Signora Marchesa and believe in the

Continuing admiration of your devoted,

Andrea de' Ricasoli

JACOB SCHRETTER'S HAND

August 13

Yesterday, leaving the Town Council after long deliber-
ations about the Red Flux—most certainly a powerful ally
of the Turks—I encountered Schabeyssen, who recited to
me at least ten different prescriptions against the disease,
Acherontic concoctions, all, of useless weeds. He also talked
of fumigation. This, along with boiling the water, seems to
help, i.e., if you fumigate the house and the belongings of
the stricken (as we learned in '79). But it makes no sense to
fumigate the patient, as those quacks have people do. They
have the poor sick hung up by their arms and legs (like so
many hams in the chimney) over a wood fire spiced with
cloves, allegedly to smoke out the evil. I would like to forbid
this practice in town, even though it would attract me the
hostility of those pill mixers, but it only could be done by
consent of the Town Council and there are many who
swear by Schabeyssen's ways. Would that Redi were here to
help us separate the quacks' superstition from true and
proven medicine, although I would not wish this foul air on
him. Yet he probably would not mind too much; he is the
most iron-stomached man I ever met, a true scientist and Ci-
mentoso.

August 16

This morning I went up into St. Stephen's tower and looked
through Starhemberg's spyglass. We saw the Grand Vizier
being carried into the trenches in an iron-clad litter, inspect-

ing the work of the sappers. Starhemberg says that he has been informed by his spies that the Sultan is dissatisfied with the progress of the siege and that Kara Mustafa had better take the city within a fortnight or his head would be forfeited. "It would look good at the end of a pike," Starhemberg added.

August 17

A prize of a hundred florins is offered to anyone who would undertake to pass through the Turkish camp to bring a message to the Duke of Lorraine. Alas, a hundred florins seem too paltry a price for attempting such a feat. No one came forward.

BARBARA SCHRETTER, IN INNSBRUCK, TO HER MOTHER,
BRIGITTA WIDOW CAMMERLOHER, IN SALZBURG

This August 18, A.D. 1683

Dear Mother:

I thank you for your letter. Pray forgive me for not having answered it sooner. I felt somewhat weak these last days, from the heat I think.

Margaret is taking good care of me; she and Cathrin also help the Monsignor's cook, who is rather old and welcomes a little relief.

As soon as we have some rain I shall write you a longer letter.

Your loving daughter,
Barbara

Pray do not let them bleed you too much.

❧

JACOB SCHRETTER'S HAND

August 22

Last night our Balthazar covered himself with glory. When I came into the house around ten, the cat, instead of sitting in my chair and greeting me with a sleepy wink, was restless and kept running to the cellar door. At first I did not pay attention to him, weary as I was; but, as he would not desist and in all appearance wanted me to follow him, I complied. All was quiet save for the continuous rumbling of the pieces, but to this we are so accustomed by now that one has to strain the ear to notice the sound at all. By the light of my candle I looked at the cellar door, but saw nothing out of the ordinary, when suddenly a little gust of wind blew out my candle. I found myself in the blackest darkness and began to grope my way upstairs again, when I perceived the thinnest gleam of light under the cellar door. I put my ear against it, and, sure enough, I could hear ever so faint a scraping noise from the other side of the door. By God, it seemed that those accursed Turks had dug a tunnel all the way from the counterscarp right to our cellar—any cellar— and were ready to emerge into the middle of town, just like the late Ulysses with his treacherous companions. (Still I do not believe that they wanted to blow up the house; it is not rubble they are after, but a rich, pillageable town. This also is the reason Kara Mustafa hesitates to storm the place. His greed is greater than his craving for glory.) However that may be, there I was, alone save for the company of the cat and, for all I knew, facing a horde of Turks at any minute.

I climbed back as fast as I could and summoned a few neighbors who were not on duty on the bastion. We went into the cellar, carrying muskets, knifes, and morning stars. By the light of the torches I opened the door. They threw themselves forward, but there was no one. They began to laugh at me, and you may believe that I felt like a fool. But then I beheld Balthazar, who had followed us. The cat ran into a corner of the cellar and sat down like, well, like a cat before a mouse hole. I walked over to him, held my torch to the wall, and there was a hole in the loose dirt under the bricks, about two feet in diameter and slanting downward. It could not have been dug more than a couple of hours be- fore. We closed it, packing it tight with sand, dirt, and bricks. The Turks, who must have heard the commotion, obviously had retreated into their tunnel. Now we have a dozen men in the cellar, watching the hole around the clock.

Starhemberg, to whom I related this, said that he would have the cat honorably mentioned in tomorrow's Order of the Day.

August 23

Another messenger from the Imperials has swum the Danube. What a relief it must have been in this heat and what pleasure to have one's lice washed away.

He has brought another letter from the Duke, promising help. The Duke is merely waiting for the Polish King to join him within two weeks. Can we hold out that long? The Turkish cannons are getting at us from the outside and the Red Flux from the inside. It is said, however, that the Turks are suffering from the same affliction, furthermore their stupid Tartars have burned all the crops in the fields around Vienna. It is therefore not easy for them to feed this huge army with provisions brought in from Hungary and Moldavia. Yet, sick or not, they keep shooting at us and digging their tunnels.

These may well be our last days; and as a man whose end could be near it befits me to set down my will and some thoughts I deem important. How does it read, then, the preamble to the testament of a God-fearing man? (I should know, I used to draw them up by the dozen):

". . . being of sick body, but, thanks to the Lord, of whole wit and reason, I leave this Vale of Tears without regret . . ."

Dear Barbara, it would not do. Primo, I am not of sick

105

body, not yet anyway. Thinner to be sure, but my innards are holding up so far, and the heat, mirabile dictu, is beneficial to my gout. Secundo, who am I to declare that I am of whole wit and reason? These last weeks have shaken stouter minds than mine. To what purpose does God send us the Turkish Plague? To punish us for our sins? That is Pater Anselmus's answer; he advanced this opinion four years ago, at the time of the Great Pestilence. I told him then that if the sickness was indeed God's punishment for our sins, we would be covered with boils our whole life long. Does He bring these afflictions upon us to test our mettle? Does He use the heathens as an instrument of His wrath, as He uses the Antichrist? Or does He avert His face and deliver us to our free will, Christian and heathen alike? Such thoughts are none too comfortable; yet I shall not shirk from following their course. It leads me to more questions, further uncertainty, and, yes, to doubt. But what would faith be, were it not to be conquered from doubt? Doubt is to faith what night is to day, what sorrow is to joy. Sorrow refreshes joy, doubt refreshes faith. Without God's will no sparrow falls from the roof. We shall see whether my doubt will help me to believe this with all my heart. Amen.

As for the Vale of Tears—I did not walk through it. Born at Innsbruck, a town the Great War had by-passed, I grew up without ever having smelled the smoke from burning houses. I never had to run the gauntlet; no Swedish Drink was ever poured down my throat. My school days were happy. I had friends; I traveled. I have seen the wine-dark sea, St. Peter's dome, the thousand masts in the port of Amsterdam. My mind was keen. I studied diligently at the University, but I can say also that I learned much from conversations in taverns with men of all trades. I delighted in the works of Homer and Vergil. Music was my joy and solace. I never have known want or sickness (except for my gout to which I am now so accustomed that I truly miss it whenever I feel free from it). Lastly, God in His goodness has given me you, Barbara, and the hope of a son. Therefore, if I must die, I shall leave this world, Turks and all, with great regret indeed.

Dear Barbara, if God grants us this child, bring him up in honesty and cheerfulness. I shall write no longish memorandum for you—Kirnsperger will stand by you as long as he lives, and, I am sure, Magalotti will gladly counsel you as to the boy's schooling. One thing, though, you must take to heart: Do not ever tolerate cruelty. Let our son be a spendthrift, a womanizer, for all I care (though I would be far from pleased), but cruelty is a coward's sport.

One hour after Angelus.

Three shells have torn a hole into the Castle Bastion. We filled it with tables, chests, doors, iron window grills—there was even a wine press thrown in!

Whatever happens, stay in Innsbruck. If the Turks take us, there will be no more to be said and it would be a miracle if these papers ever came into your hands at all. If relief comes in time and I should be dead, the deed to the house is filed away in the Town Archives, together with my will, which makes you and the child heirs to my possessions. God bless you both.

August 28

A thunderstorm gave us some respite from the Turkish shells.

107

ANDREA DE' RICASOLI, AT FLORENCE, TO GIOVANNI DE'
GUALDI, IN CARE OF THE HOUSE OF FERONI, BRANCH AT
INNSBRUCK, WITH A GOLD-AND-LEATHER–BOUND EDITION
OF THE *DECAMERON*

This August 28, 1683

My dear Giovanni:

May I presume a favor of your friendship?

The enclosed volume is to be passed silentissime into the hands of Margaret, servant at St. Mary's new presbyterium. The said Margaret has seen six decades at least but is as alert as a weasel. Every night she accompanies her mistress to Vespers at St. Anne's. Sapienti sat.

All my thanks and the assurance that you may count on me should you ever need a similar service performed.

Salve atque vale.

Your Andrea

Went to Lonchio yesterday. The Marchesa kept asking about you. For how long do you have to remain yet on your Pontus?

JACOB SCHRETTER'S HAND

August 29

The Feast of St. John the Baptist. Will they storm today? It is quite possible, for they set great store by the 29th of August, St. John being revered by them as a great friend of Mahomet, just as many of our saints and even the Savior have found their way into the Koran, albeit in the most curious mummery. However that may be, this date several times has been a lamentable memory for us Christians. Byzantium was conquered on that day and King Louis II was beaten at Mohács. The Turks know it as well as we do. We have reinforced the number of men on the bastions and pulled iron chains across many streets.

A shell has decapitated the tower of the Minorites' Church.

The day is fresh and clear. As I noted, we had a thunderstorm last night, and in the early morning on the bastion I felt that autumn was not far away. We are waiting.

FROM THE RECORDS OF RUPRECHT STEINSCHNEYDER, BAILIFF OF THE COLLOREDO FIEF, ARCHBISHOPRIC OF SALZBURG

This September 5, A.D. 1683

Flogged: Axinger, Aloysius, aet. 35, for being recurrently late with tithe.

A fire in the Spinning House. All wenches recaptured, save Gerlacherin, Veronica, aet. 30, scullery maid, had stolen two silver spoons; Schützin, Caecilia, aet. 50, gravedigger's wife, had taken the silver buttons off a dead body's doublet; Kohlröser, Theresia, aet. 20, truant.

FROM THE CHRONICLE OF NICOLAUS HOCKE, TOWN CLERK AND SYNDIC OF VIENNA

6 huius

This morning the Enemy has continued his shooting and again has run against the bastion. At night we shot many rockets from St. Stephen's tower. From six o'clock in the morning until noon we have observed from said tower that the Turks are ferrying fresh troops over the Danube and that their camp is busy and full of new soldiers.

Today the Mayor, the well-born Master Andreas von Liebenberg, after having suffered five weeks of sickness and after having been comforted by the Holy Sacrament, has died in the Lord. May the Almighty God lead his soul to Eternal Joy and Bliss.

11 huius

From St. Stephen's tower we saw the Enemy move toward the hills. We also saw some troops (whom we hope to be our succor) assembled by the new and the old castles on the Kahlenberg. The said troops, as we remarked, began turning their pieces toward the town, i.e., the Enemy. More and more troops appeared on the Kahlenberg, and this furthered our hopes that these were indeed the long-desired succor. We fired three rockets and three cannon shots, the signal for His Serene Highness the Duke of Lorraine, that the Enemy is about to storm. His Excellency the Commander ordered the entire citizenry and soldatesca to stand ready.

12 Septembris

The Enemy continued to throw bombs and grenades, and this more vehemently than ever. He also furthered the mining work most zealously so that we altogether believed and expected him to blow up the mines which had been laid by the Castle Bastion. However we observed the Christian Armada and the very much longed-for succor descend from the old and the new castles on the Kahlenberg, regiment after regiment, continuously firing their pieces at the Enemy. By noon they had come down and moved forth into the vineyards, where the Enemy had aligned his troops. But said succor, in best and splendid battle order, contended with the Turks most heatedly. By four o'clock in the afternoon the Enemy was pushed back into his own camp, receding always and in such confusion that he finally turned tail and took to flight. Thus the Christian Armada not only won the day, but the Enemy's provisions, ammunition, pieces, tents, and baggage as well.

Meanwhile, notwithstanding the battle at the foot of the Kahlenberg and in the vineyards, the Enemy still continued his shelling of the town — no day during the whole Siege has seen so much firing — and for this the citizenry and the soldatesca stood good and ready.

We shelled the Turkish trenches without respite; nevertheless the Enemy still fired his pieces at the town, most of all at St. Stephen's tower, and this until the last moment, as if the Turkish Army still had the advantage. Moreover, as soon as they beheld Christian troops at their back, they turned their pieces around and fired at the succor. It was only after the Janissars had been bested that the Turks ran from the trenches, abandoning their camp altogether, with pieces, provisions, weapons, carts, oxen, bulls, horses, and other cattle in uncountable numbers. After the Enemy had been driven to flight and could

not be chased further on account of nightfall, the soldatesca began pillaging the camp. The Poles seized the
Grand Vizier's tent and a few other fair-sized ones,
wherein they found an immense treasure of gold, precious stones, jewelry, silver coins, and rich garments.
They also got the Grand Vizier's war chest with his secret papers and the green silken standard of Mahomet.

13 Septembris

This day the townsfolk in great numbers ran out through
the city gates to have a look at the Enemy's trenches.
The latter are huge, deep and intertwined, a labyrinth of
ditches. These said ditches were reinforced by scaffolding
of wooden beams and covered with boards, dirt, and
woolen sacks so that neither shells nor grenades could

damage them. The bulwark between the Castle and the Löwel bastions was dug through and through as if, Salva Venia, pigs had been burrowing there.

In the camp we beheld a great number of dead cattle, horses, oxen, and camels, also many slain Turks and Christians, but, above all (and this could have moved even a stony heart to pity), many innocent little children lying about and some of them still alive. His Episcopal Grace, Monsignor Count Leopold Kollonitsch, had them gathered up, brought into town, fed, and sheltered. He will have them decently raised at his cost.

14 Septembris

Today His Majesty the King of Poland and His Serene Highness the Duke of Lorraine rode into town accompanied by His Excellency the Commander and many gentlemen of the Nobility. The whole Citizenry was aligned to greet His Majesty and His Serene Highness. They visited the church of the Patrum Jesuitorum, and then, with uncovered heads, His Majesty and His Serene Highness rode over to St. Stephen's Church to be received there by the entire Chapter and many folk.

Thus this grievous Siege, which had lasted sixty-two days (this is almost nine weeks), came to an end through GOD'S mercy by intercession of the Holy Mother of God, the Most Illustrious House of Austria, and the town's two Patron Saints, to wit, St. Joseph and St. Leopold.

What plight this (now lifted) Siege had been to the townsfolk and what joy and jubilation this day has brought them who are now freed with their kith and kin from Turkish cruelty and slavery, no one can tell better than I and all those of us who suffered it.

113

NICOLAUS HOCKE, DOCTOR UTRIUSQUE IURIS, CLERK AND
SYNDIC OF THE TOWN OF VIENNA, TO THE WELL-BORN MISTRESS
BARBARA SCHRETTER, SPOUSE OF THE WELL-BORN MASTER
JACOB SCHRETTER, IMPERIAL COUNCILOR AND MEMBER OF THE
WORTHY TOWN COUNCIL OF VIENNA

This Septembris 15, A.D. 1683

Worthy and Gracious Mistress Barbara Schretterin:
Whereas, through the mercy of GOD and through the arms
of His Majesty Emperor Leopold I, Gratia Dei, and through
the arms of His Majesty King John I Sobieski of Poland and
through the arms of His Serene Highness Duke Charles of
Lorraine this Town of Vienna has been relieved of the Turkish Scourge on the Twelfth Day Septembris A.D. 1683, and

Whereas today the Taxis Mail is setting forth from the
said Town with dispatches for His Eminence the Arch-
bishop-Cardinal of Salzburg and for His Serene Highness
Duke Leopold of Tyrol in Innsbruck, I avail myself of this
opportunity to send you the enclosed papers which Jacob
Schretter, on the 1 huius (the day when, afflicted with the
Red Flux, he was taken to the Passauerhof), entrusted to me
with the earnest entreaty to have them surrendered into
your hands at my earliest convenience, should this town,
with GOD'S help, be freed from the Arch-Enemy's grasp.

> Your Well-born Grace's devoted servant,
> Nicolaus Hocke, Dr. u.i.
> Town Clerk and Syndic of Vienna

POST SCRIPTUM

His Grace, Bishop Leopold Count Kollonitsch, upon visiting
the Passauerhof and discovering Master Schretter there, has

114

October 21

Yesterday His Grace, Bishop Kollonitsch, called on Jacob. When I came home from the green market (I go there with Margaret every day to make sure that we get the best for Jacob), I found the Bishop sitting by my husband's bed. He greeted me most pleasantly and said that now he had not the slightest doubt that Jacob would recover, and I thanked him for having taken my husband out of the Passauerhof.

Then they talked some and the Bishop said that the Emperor did not wish to resume residence in Vienna as long as the Castle was not thoroughly repaired. "This is indeed what I had expected," said Jacob, and I related what our boatman had said, namely, that the Emperor had shed tears at the sight of all the ruin, and the Bishop replied that tears were all we ever got from His Majesty.

"Carolus Quintus is turning in his coffin," I said (recalling what Monsignor Kirnsperger would always mutter whenever there was talk about the Emperor), and His Grace laughed out loud, saying to my husband that he did not know that he, Jacob, had such a spirited wife and that if I had stayed in Town, they might have chased the Turk even sooner. Then, seeing that Jacob, though pleased, looked weary, he rose and took his leave. I accompanied the Bishop to his carriage, and he told me to come and visit his orphanage, where he is sheltering about two hundred little children which were found in the Turkish Camp, and I promised to come and bring food and clothing for them.

Dear Mother, pray do not worry yourself about us. With God's help we will all be well.

Could you give my regards to Burgl and to the Aichbichler boys.

> I kiss your hands,
> Your obedient daughter,
> Barbara

✦§§✦

JACOB SCHRETTER, IN VIENNA, TO MONSIGNOR MICHAEL
KIRNSPERGER, IN INNSBRUCK (DICTATED — BARBARA'S HAND)

This October 18, A.D. 1683

My Dear Reverend Friend:

God in His goodness has given me great happiness: My wife
has safely reached Vienna, hale and healthy notwithstanding her long wearying journey.

As for my sickness — I begin to recover from it, slowly but
steadily.

Reports of the Battle and of the relief of our Town must
have reached Innsbruck by now, but as I am very weary I
shall save for next time the detailed account of those events.
Suffice it to say that even in my fever, lying among the sick
and half-dead in the Passauerhof, I could hear the bells, the
cannon shots, and the cheering outside in the streets, and I
said my Nunc dimittis with a grateful heart.

I thank you again for the steadfast love you have lavished
upon Barbara and me in tempore calamitatis.

> Your devoted and grateful friend,
> Jacob Schretter

BARBARA SCHRETTER, IN VIENNA, TO HER MOTHER, BRIGITTA
WIDOW CAMMERLOHER, IN SALZBURG

On the Fifth of November, in the Year of the Lord 1683

My Dear Mother:

I have not heard from you in more than a month and am worrying about your health. Pray let me know how you are.

As for me, I am feeling well, thanks to the Good Lord. Margaret put three drops of Holy Water on my breasts; if it runs off, she said, I will have a boy; if it stays, a girl. It ran down (as I had expected it would), and Margaret was pleased. (I will also be happy with a girl.)

The child is kicking and does not let me sleep nights, but I do not mind; I thank God every day, for He has been good to me. It has been a sorrowful summer, but He gave me strength to go through it. I have many blessings left for which to be thankful, as was shown to me again last night.

As I came home from Vigil, Margaret told me to come straight to the kitchen. I went and there I saw a woman sitting by the hearth. Margaret had only one candle going and the embers gave not much light either, so I could hardly make her out at first. But then she stood up and said, "Barbara, do you still know me?" It was Thresl. I took her in my arms and in all my pity and surprise I had to laugh a little, for we are both far gone with child and could not embrace properly. I told Margaret to bring more candles so I could see my friend's face. She has not changed much save that she is quite sunburned. She wore a twill skirt and bodice with many patches, a kerchief around her head, and wooden clogs on her bare feet. Her feet were all red with cold and her hands were also red and had calluses all over.

Dearest Mother, I now have to confess to you that for the last three weeks I have known what has happened to Thresl.

When you told me in September that Thresl had moved away with Straihamer and that you had not seen her mother for a good while, I guessed something to be amiss from your words. Therefore on our way toward the Linzer Gate I halted at the Kohlröser house and found it locked. I worked the door knocker rather loudly, and this got some neighbors to look out of their windows to see who made such a commotion, among them the Lechner Ploni, who came down and told me the story straight away. She also said that the Kohlröserin had left town and that the house was being put up for sale.

I know that you kept all this from me so as not to upset me, but I would have learned about it anyway, for last week I was sorting out some of Jacob's clothes and your letter fell out of his coat pocket. I saw your handwriting and Thresl's name on it, and curiosity got the better of me. Pray forgive me and do not hold it against me.

Thresl told me that she had worked in the fields until the wife of a farmer recognized her and chased her away. She then walked for twenty miles, hoping to find work farther away from Salzburg, when she was seized as a truant by the men from the Colloredo Fief. They put her in the Spinning House, where she had to work from dawn to dusk. The night of the fire she ran away, hiding by day and walking by night; and when she finally was outside the Bishopric she worked again mainly as a scullery maid in several taverns, and after the Turks' retreat she set out for Vienna, working and starving, and finally made it to our house.

I said that she could stay with us and that Margaret was to

122

ordered him to be brought back to his house and has two Fratres Capucinos tend to his needs, which are few, as he is of great weakness, though, through GOD'S mercy, he does not lose his, Salva Venia, innards any longer.

The same.

ᴥᶘᶘᴥ

GIOVANNI DE' GUALDI, IN INNSBRUCK, TO ANDREA DE' RICASOLI, AT FLORENCE

September 28, 1683

My twice-fortunate Andrea:

Your Boccaccio (where did you obtain this exquisite edition?) is in the hands of the efficacious Margaret.

The very day I received the little package, I went to St. Anne's. According to schedule, the obiter dicta emerged from the church after Vespers. Favored by the night I gave her the book and even succeeded in talking to her for two moments. I was lucky indeed to catch her: She revealed to me that her mistress was preparing to travel to Vienna within the next two days because she (Signora Schretter) had received a pack of letters from there informing her of her husband's grave illness. (Apparently Schretter had caught the Red Flux, that affliction common to the besieged. Dulce et decorum pro patria mori, but pro patria cacare?)

Margaret was rather indignant at being subjected to the rigors of such a precipitate journey (". . . and what for? He's probably dead by now. I saw it in my cards!"), but her mistress seems to be rather strong-willed and also to have the approval and encouragement of the old Deacon.

115

The next day curiosity prevailed upon me to see the face that made you go to such lengths as to buy this most fancy tome. She came out of the church and in the full moon I had a good look at her. Fortunate Andrea! And twice fortunate for having succeeded in disentangling yourself, apparently without too much damage, from the fetters of those red-golden tresses. For—I have to tell you, you had a narrow escape indeed. Read and tremble: Margaret revealed to me that Signora Schretter, after coming home from the Black Swan, had been weeping inconsolably and confessed that, had you made the slightest move toward her, she would not have had the strength to leave.

Recommend me to your father, to the Count and to the most enchanting Marchesa. I'll kiss her feet, her hands, and whatever else she will be generous enough to abandon to my ministrations as soon as I come back from the Hyperboreans, which should be by the end of October.

Salve atque vale.

Your Giovanni de' Gualdi

BARBARA SCHRETTER, IN VIENNA, TO HER MOTHER, BRIGITTA WIDOW CAMMERLOHER, IN SALZBURG

This October 15, A.D. 1683

My Dear Mother:
The Taxis Mail going only on Mondays, I have time for a longer letter.

I have arrived safely and found Jacob alive, thank the Good Lord, although in great weakness.

As we drove through the Schotten Gate toward our house I grew very anxious and even more so when we reached it, for we saw all windows closed and all shutters drawn. Yet the door proved to be unlocked. I entered, and though I heard somebody busying himself in the kitchen I went straight up to the bedroom and there Jacob was lying in the bed, so thin and wan that I scarcely believed he could be alive. He opened his eyes and recognized me and tried to reach out for my hand, but was too weak, and when I took his hand in mine it was nothing but thin bones.

Presently one of the Capuchins came in (I learned a little later that His Grace, Bishop Kollonitsch, had ordered two of them to take care of Jacob). He was pleased indeed and said that Jacob was recovering and that he had been far worse (which is hardly thinkable) and that now with the help of God and with me here my husband surely would get well again.

This was three days ago and, truly, he gets a little better every day. He can keep some food down now, oatmeal and egg yolks mostly. Tomorrow we might try chicken broth to give him some strength. Yesterday Schabeyssen, the Town Surgeon, called, but Jacob, though feeble, is thoroughly clearheaded and said that he did not want to try any of Schabeyssen's medicines — now less than ever, since God in His mercy is giving him back his life, the Turks are beaten, and he is again together with me.

Jacob tries to talk, but it wearies him and I tell him that he should rest and that we will have time for tales when he is stronger. Then he asks me to talk to him and tell things about Innsbruck, and I speak to him for a while, about Monsignor Kirnsperger, of whom he is quite fond, and after a while he falls asleep. He is nothing but skin and bones but, strangely, looks younger in his sickness.

Although Margaret and Cathrin are now here, the Capuchins do not want to leave; they have grown fond of Jacob and vie to make him comfortable. They even shave him every second day.

We are not troubled for food, the Turks, people tell me, having left many provisions. However, this year's harvest is lost and it takes a while to bring in grain, flour, barley, and the like from the south. We have enough meat, but everything is dear.

The journey was easy. It took us no more than three days to get from Salzburg to Linz. At Linz I sent Vitus ahead with the carriage, to wait for us in Klosterneuburg, and we traveled by boat, which was more comfortable. As we passed Tulln we saw all the land around burned, not only houses, barns, and churches, but crops as well. The boatman told us that the Emperor, when visiting the town after the siege, also came by way of the river and wept when he saw the devastation.

October 19

I am taking up this letter today, as Jacob had called for me while I was writing. He had slept very well and wanted me to write down a letter to Monsignor Kirnsperger, for he is still too weak to sit up, let alone to hold a quill. Yet he is getting better all the time. Today he ate two eggs with a little toasted bread and kept everything down very well.

October 21

Yesterday His Grace, Bishop Kollonitsch, called on Jacob. When I came home from the green market (I go there with Margaret every day to make sure that we get the best for Jacob), I found the Bishop sitting by my husband's bed. He greeted me most pleasantly and said that now he had not the slightest doubt that Jacob would recover, and I thanked him for having taken my husband out of the Passauerhof.

Then they talked some and the Bishop said that the Emperor did not wish to resume residence in Vienna as long as the Castle was not thoroughly repaired. "This is indeed what I had expected," said Jacob, and I related what our boatman had said, namely, that the Emperor had shed tears at the sight of all the ruin, and the Bishop replied that tears were all we ever got from His Majesty.

"Carolus Quintus is turning in his coffin," I said (recalling what Monsignor Kirnsperger would always mutter whenever there was talk about the Emperor), and His Grace laughed out loud, saying to my husband that he did not know that he, Jacob, had such a spirited wife and that if I had stayed in Town, they might have chased the Turk even sooner. Then, seeing that Jacob, though pleased, looked weary, he rose and took his leave. I accompanied the Bishop to his carriage, and he told me to come and visit his orphanage, where he is sheltering about two hundred little children which were found in the Turkish Camp, and I promised to come and bring food and clothing for them.

Dear Mother, pray do not worry yourself about us. With God's help we will all be well.

Could you give my regards to Burgl and to the Aichbichler boys.

I kiss your hands,
Your obedient daughter,
Barbara

◄§§►

JACOB SCHRETTER, IN VIENNA, TO MONSIGNOR MICHAEL
KIRNSPERGER, IN INNSBRUCK (DICTATED — BARBARA'S HAND)

This October 18, A.D. 1683

My Dear Reverend Friend:
God in His goodness has given me great happiness: My wife
has safely reached Vienna, hale and healthy notwithstanding her long wearying journey.

As for my sickness—I begin to recover from it, slowly but
steadily.

Reports of the Battle and of the relief of our Town must
have reached Innsbruck by now, but as I am very weary I
shall save for next time the detailed account of those events.
Suffice it to say that even in my fever, lying among the sick
and half-dead in the Passauerhof, I could hear the bells, the
cannon shots, and the cheering outside in the streets, and I
said my Nunc dimittis with a grateful heart.

I thank you again for the steadfast love you have lavished
upon Barbara and me in tempore calamitatis.

Your devoted and grateful friend,
Jacob Schretter

BARBARA SCHRETTER, IN VIENNA, TO HER MOTHER, BRIGITTA
WIDOW CAMMERLOHER, IN SALZBURG

On the Fifth of November, in the Year of the Lord 1683

My Dear Mother:

I have not heard from you in more than a month and am worrying about your health. Pray let me know how you are.

As for me, I am feeling well, thanks to the Good Lord. Margaret put three drops of Holy Water on my breasts; if it runs off, she said, I will have a boy; if it stays, a girl. It ran down (as I had expected it would), and Margaret was pleased. (I will also be happy with a girl.)

The child is kicking and does not let me sleep nights, but I do not mind; I thank God every day, for He has been good to me. It has been a sorrowful summer, but He gave me strength to go through it. I have many blessings left for which to be thankful, as was shown to me again last night.

As I came home from Vigil, Margaret told me to come straight to the kitchen. I went and there I saw a woman sitting by the hearth. Margaret had only one candle going and the embers gave not much light either, so I could hardly make her out at first. But then she stood up and said, "Barbara, do you still know me?" It was Thresl. I took her in my arms and in all my pity and surprise I had to laugh a little, for we are both far gone with child and could not embrace properly. I told Margaret to bring more candles so I could see my friend's face. She has not changed much save that she is quite sunburned. She wore a twill skirt and bodice with many patches, a kerchief around her head, and wooden clogs on her bare feet. Her feet were all red with cold and her hands were also red and had calluses all over.

121

Dearest Mother, I now have to confess to you that for the last three weeks I have known what has happened to Thresl.

When you told me in September that Thresl had moved away with Straihamer and that you had not seen her mother for a good while, I guessed something to be amiss from your words. Therefore on our way toward the Linzer Gate I halted at the Kohlröser house and found it locked. I worked the door knocker rather loudly, and this got some neighbors to look out of their windows to see who made such a commotion, among them the Lechner Ploni, who came down and told me the story straight away. She also said that the Kohlröserin had left town and that the house was being put up for sale.

I know that you kept all this from me so as not to upset me, but I would have learned about it anyway, for last week I was sorting out some of Jacob's clothes and your letter fell out of his coat pocket. I saw your handwriting and Thresl's name on it, and curiosity got the better of me. Pray forgive me and do not hold it against me.

Thresl told me that she had worked in the fields until the wife of a farmer recognized her and chased her away. She then walked for twenty miles, hoping to find work farther away from Salzburg, when she was seized as a truant by the men from the Colloredo Fief. They put her in the Spinning House, where she had to work from dawn to dusk. The night of the fire she ran away, hiding by day and walking by night; and when she finally was outside the Bishopric she worked again mainly as a scullery maid in several taverns, and after the Turks' retreat she set out for Vienna, working and starving, and finally made it to our house.

I said that she could stay with us and that Margaret was to

122

have the little garret chamber readied for her. Margaret shook her head and said I should wait to hear whether my husband would allow it. I told her to mind her own business and to do as I said, but inside I was quite worried, since truly I did not know how he would look at it. I said a prayer and went upstairs.

When I approached his bed, he said, "Why don't you bring her in?" (Margaret must have told him on the spot.) So I went back into the kitchen and fetched Thresl. She entered the sickroom with me and hardly dared look at him. But he held out his hand to her and said, "Welcome." At this Thresl began weeping so much that she could not answer and I cried too. He said that he was not dying and therefore did not need two weeping women around his bed and why not bring him some chicken broth as soon as we had dried up a little.

So Thresl is staying with us. She is a great help to Margaret and Cathrin, and her child does not seem to bother her too much. Her hair has grown back to almost six inches, and Margaret has trimmed it all around. Thresl now looks like one of the Emperor's pages, which is strange to behold, for you see a boy's head on the body of a very pregnant woman. She does not like this look and says she will wear a kerchief until she can plait her hair again.

She kisses your hands and asks if you would be good enough to tell her mother that she is safe, as she dares not to write herself since she does not know whether her mother has forgiven her.

I pray God to keep and protect you, Dearest Mother.

Your obedient daughter,
Barbara
123

ALMANAC — BARBARA SCHRETTER'S HAND

While Going With Child (from Sister Consolatio)

Take fennel, honey, saffron, and white wine. Bring to a boil, drink as warm as you can. It strengthens the fruit of the womb. Also to be taken after great fright or fatigue.

Against the itching of the breasts:

New clay softened with water. Drench a piece of linen in it, put it on the breasts. It helps.

MONSIGNOR MICHAEL KIRNSPERGER, DEACON OF ST. MARY'S IN INNSBRUCK, TO JACOB SCHRETTER, IN VIENNA

This November 6, Anno Salutis Nostrae 1683

My Dear Friend:

Need I tell you with what joy I received your letter, so diligently. penned by your good wife? God is merciful indeed. Barbara surely is taking excellent care of you, and, God willing, we will see each other again when you have recovered from this grievous illness.

If we have heard about the Battle and about the Great Victory! There was talk of nothing else. By now some of the volunteers have returned, and therefore we are fortunate enough to learn about the Triumph of the Christian Arms from those who were there.

God's blessing to all—the glorious Captains, His Majesty the King of Poland, the Duke of Lorraine, the brave solda-tesca, the no-less-brave citizenry, Starhemberg and Kollo-nitsch—to the latter my brotherly greetings. It grieves me that I cannot include His Majesty the Emperor in this paean; would that Carolus Quintus were still alive. He would have led his troops into battle and brought increased glory to the House of Austria.

Can we ever praise God enough who has freed us from the Turkish Scourge? Let us pray that this was their last as-sault and that your children (if God grants them to you) will be spared such a trial. Est in votis.

As for myself, I am of good cheer, but suffering from a persistent dry cough. I am advised to have some thorough bleeding done to me, but I am hesitant. Due to weak veins, I always lose more of the precious fluid than others do. The Theophrastians are in favor of radical bleeding, but such a purge seems disquieting to me.

Dear friend, I send you my blessings, both to you and your dear wife. She was a joy to have around when she dwelled in my house.

Salvete atque valete.

Salutem in Christo,
Michael Kirnsperger

BRIGITTA CAMMERLOHER, WIDOW, IN SALZBURG, TO HER
DAUGHTER, BARBARA SCHRETTER, IN VIENNA

This November 20, A.D. 1683

Dear Daughter:

I received both your letters. I thank the Good Lord for holding His hand over you and your husband.

As for Thresl, since the fat is in the fire, you might as well
tell her that her mother has gone back to Schwarzach to live
with her own folks and that Straihamer has bought the
house for a third of its worth and has won his lawsuit.

Also tell her that she should not ever come back here, as
Steinschneyder, the new Colloredo bailiff, is looking for her
everywhere. Let Jacob know of this—otherwise he might
buy a bucketful of troubles for himself if they ever find out
that he shelters a runaway from the Spin House. (And find
out they will; trust a blabbermouth such as Ploni.)

Write to me about all this. I am greatly worried and also
worried that Thresl might come to grief again if ever she be
caught.

Tell her that I will try to send word to her mother that
she is out of trouble and mischief, at least for the next few
days.

God be with all of you.

Your devoted mother,
Brigitta Cammerloherin, Widow

JACOB SCHRETTER, IN VIENNA, TO MONSIGNOR MICHAEL
KIRNSPERGER, DEACON OF ST. MARY'S IN INNSBRUCK

This November 21, A.D. 1683

My Dear and Learned Friend:

Many thanks for your most welcome letter of November the
6th. As you can see, I am not writing manu propria. My
stomach gets braver by the hour; yesterday it successfully
took in three bites of cooked chicken, and so we proceed,
thanks to God, lente autem sicure.

Last week we had an excellent St. Martin's goose of which
I did not partake, except through my enchanted nose. The
cook was—incredibile dictu—the Kohlröser girl who had
come to our house in a sad shape indeed. She is most visibly
pregnant—by the younger Kuenburg, fama sufficiente, and
has left Salzburg after a most unpleasant session with the
Provost. We took her in. Christ forgave the Adulteress—so I
could do no less, all the more as she did not put any horns
on *my* head. And old Straihamer would have richly deserved such a ready-made crown had she been lucky enough
to catch him in time, for patrem quem nuptiae demonstrant.

As for her child, I am more sanguine in this point than
most folks are. Carolus Quintus of Glorious Memory had a
son by an innkeeper's daughter who did not turn out badly.
If young Kuenburg does half as well by Thresl there will be
no cause for recriminations. Besides, she is a strong and diligent girl, a far better cook than old Margaret, and good company for my wife.

I am sending you a little barrel of new wine. I do as the

Ancients did, who never opened a barrel before fermentation was complete. They were not such pigs as our countryfolk are, who gulp down the must as soon as it squirts out from under the press, yeast crumbs and all, no matter how murky it may look, and afterward suffer the torments of Hell from their kidney stones.

Yesterday Barbara went to St. Anne's with my old coat, following St. Martin's example, only better: She gave away the whole coat. Date et dabitur vobis, said the Lord.

May God keep you in good cheer.

Your devoted friend,
Jacobus Schretter

❦

RUPRECHT STEINSCHNEYDER, BAILIFF OF THE COLLOREDO FIEF IN SALZBURG, TO JACOB SCHRETTER VON SCHRETTENBERG, TOWN COUNCILOR IN VIENNA

This November 22, A.D. 1683

Your Honor:

It is my duty to write to Your Honor in regard to a certain woman, Kohlröser Theresia Elisabeth, aet. 20. Said woman after having been flogged in due process of Law and after having been fined 50 florins for illicit commerce with a known witch and angel-maker has been apprehended as a truant and appropriated to the Colloredo Fief as an indentured servant. For repeated disobedience said woman was put in the Spin House. The night the said Spin House burned down, the said woman escaped.

Your Honor is being suspected of giving shelter to the said woman. Your Honor is herewith earnestly enjoined to return the said woman, Kohlröser Theresia Elisabeth, to her lawful proprietor, His Excellency Count Ferdinand Colloredo.

Given at Salzburg, this November 22, A.D. 1683

Your obedient servant,
Ruprecht Steinschneyder, Bailiff

◄§§►

JACOB SCHRETTER, TOWN COUNCILOR IN VIENNA, TO RUPRECHT STEINSCHNEYDER, BAILIFF OF THE COLLOREDO FIEF IN SALZBURG

30 November A.D. 1683

I accuse receipt of Yours of 22 huius, A.D. 1683.

The woman in question, Kohlröser Theresia Elisabeth, aet. 20, is indeed living at my house.

Whatever her recent circumstances as an indentured servant to the Colloredo Fief might have been, it probably has escaped your attention that after the abatement of the Plague A.D. 1679 (for which we thank the Almighty) the Town of Vienna has been declared Asylum to any fugitive from the Secular Arm (barring murder) for 5 (five) years, by resolution of His Apostolic Majesty, Emperor Leopold I (whom God may preserve).

Given this 30 November A.D. 1683 in the Good Town of Vienna and sealed by me.

Jacobus Schretter von Schrettenberg,
Town Councilor

BARBARA SCHRETTER, IN VIENNA, TO HER MOTHER, BRIGITTA
WIDOW CAMMERLOHER, IN SALZBURG

This November the Thirtieth, A.D. 1683

My Dear Mother:

Last week Thresl gave birth to a little daughter. Her name is
Brigitta Jacoba. Thresl wanted these names to be given to
her child in honor of you and of my husband, who have
been so good to her. She said she also would have liked to
name the little girl after me, but then she thought that three
names might have looked presumptuous on a poor bastard
girl, and I said that I understood and that I was happy anyway because the little one looked healthy and pretty.

Thresl is not in a good vein right now, as the delivery was
not easy. It began last Sunday. We had already gone to bed,
Jacob and I, when I heard a scream and then another one.
This last one sounded as if she were biting into the bedsheet. I threw on a few clothes and went upstairs. (Jacob
who often suffers from sleeplessness did not even wake up
this time.) Margaret was already there and had lit a candle.
Thresl was lying quite still, and I thought maybe it had just
been a nightmare when she was seized by a cramp. She bit
into her bedsheet, and I told her to scream if she felt like it
and had Cathrin run for the midwife.

Margaret went down to warm some water for a cataplasm.
I said this would never do, what with all this running up
and down and told her to wake Vitus so he could help us.
He came and with much grumbling carried Thresl down the
stairs into Margaret's room, which is next to the kitchen,
and laid her down on the bed. It was cold in there, so Margaret brought a coal basin and lit the coals. They smoked a
lot but made the room a trifle warmer.

130

Thresl now had a cramp every half hour or so. In between I sat with her, holding her hand and talking to her, and she remembered many things from the time when we were children in Salzburg. In the meantime the midwife arrived. Her name is Sibylla Hutterin and she is the skinniest broomstick I ever saw. She asked us first of all whether we had the stool ready.

This upset us very much, both Margaret and me, for we had entirely forgotten about it. So I sent Vitus up to the garret with a light to pull out the family birthing stool from under our old chests and chairs. He did not like this one bit and grumbled aloud, but I made him do it all the same. (I would not have made such a fuss had I known that the stool would turn out to be of no use to Thresl. Still, I am keeping it downstairs, for my own time is not too far off.) The Hutterin bade me hold the candle aloft while she was taking a look at Thresl. She felt and kneaded Thresl's belly for a while, which made the poor soul bite the bedsheets again. The Hutterin then said that the child was coming feet first, which was against nature, that there was plenty of time yet, and that she wanted some supper. Cathrin went for bread, sausage, and cake. The Hutterin also wanted warm beer and lots of it, for it would be a long night, she said. Margaret went into the cellar and brought up a whole little casket of white beer and warmed some for the Hutterin, who was eating away at the sausage as if she had been on water and bread for the last four weeks. When she had cleaned up everything to the merest crumb, she went into the kitchen and did not return. Thresl began thrashing around, the cramps coming one right after another. She was covered with sweat. I went into the kitchen to get the Hutterin and saw her there, leaning against the hearth and snoring, the beer casket almost empty. I shook her, but she would mumble only that there was still plenty of time and go back to sleep. So I had Cathrin run for Schabeyssen, the Apothecary, and also for Sister Agnes, who often tends the sick poor and knows her way around women in childbirth. Master Schabeyssen came within the hour. (Jacob does not like him at all, but I did not know whom else to call.) He had with him his apprentice, who was carrying a large chest full of medicines on his back. I told the boy to set down the chest and to wait in the kitchen. Thresl's cramps got worse, but the child would not move. Schabeyssen reached into his chest and brought out a pair of scissors. He cut off a strand of Thresl's hair, singed it over the coal basin and held it under her nose so as to make her sneeze. But she did not sneeze, only got sick from the stink. There was so much smoke in the room that at first I did not see that in the meantime Sister Agnes had come in, but not alone, for with her was Sister Consolatio. (My husband said afterward that the two together must have looked like the unlucky number 13, for Sister Agnes is quite thin and Sister Consolatio is stout.) This was a naughty thing to say, but it made me laugh. Sister Agnes told me that she also had brought Pater Anselmus (who was waiting in the hall) in case Thresl had to have Absolution, which she would sorely need, should she die, since she was bringing forth a child out of wedlock.

If she would only bring it forth, I thought, because the child still did not move. Thresl was near fainting. Schabeyssen bled her on the right thigh, so she would not choke on her own blood, he said. He drew about a pint. Presently the Hutterin came in again (she must have come to herself).

132

She kneaded Thresl's belly once more and said the child was still lying feet first and thus could not be grabbed with any forceps and Thresl had to push it out herself. With that she fastened a long rope on the bedpost and with each new cramp had Thresl pull the rope. Thresl weakened after three or four pulls, but the Hutterin said if she gave up they would have to cut her open ("As they did for Caesar," said Schabeyssen to Sister Agnes, who was warming some linen over the coal basin to give Thresl another cataplasm).

Thresl fainted. Schabeyssen went to his chest and pulled out a snakeskin. He hung it around her neck. I do not know whether it helped, but Thresl came to and pulled the rope again. I told Margaret to open the window and let the smoke out and some fresh air come in, but it soon got very cold in the room and we had to close the window again.

Master Schabeyssen said that it was a pity that Thresl was having a child out of wedlock and the child's father nowhere near, because the best help in difficult childbirth was to give the woman her husband's urine to drink (but it worked only if the man was also the father of the child). I promised myself there and then that Schabeyssen would not get near me when my time comes.

Thresl was sinking fast. She hardly could pull the rope and fell backward. Now Sister Consolatio said since Thresl could not be put on the stool as the child did not move, there was only one thing to do and the surgeon should be ready to make a good cut into the birthway as soon as she gave him the sign to do it. At this Margaret crossed herself and whispered to me that this would be the end, and ran for some brandy to give Thresl as to make her drunk and thus allow her to feel less pain. But Sister Agnes would have none of it. She said that the Lord had said, "Thou shalt bring forth thy children in woe," and that Thresl especially had to atone for her sin. This made me angry indeed, and I was about to get the brandy into Thresl myself when Sister Consolatio pushed me aside. She threw back the bed linen, spread out Thresl's legs and told Margaret and Sister Agnes each to hold one leg. Then she said to Schabeyssen, "Ready." He nodded, with his knife in his hand. Sister Consolatio said, "Now," and sat down on Thresl while Schabeyssen made a deep cut into the birthway. I never heard such a scream as came from Thresl and I hope that I will never again hear the like of it. But there was now a little leg sticking out. The Hutterin grabbed it and slowly pulled out the child, turning it a little. At first we could not even see, for all the blood, whether it was a boy or a girl. But then we saw that it was a little girl and had a Lucky Bonnet on.

The Hutterin cut the cord, spanked the child, and it cried. "This is all very well," said Schabeyssen, "but now we will have to go for the afterbirth," which he called the Secundina. He told Margaret to warm a large cut of bread. When it was ready he put it on Thresl's stomach, but it did not help. The Hutterin asked for some fine-ground pepper and held it under Thresl's nose to make her sneeze. And faint as she was, she sneezed while Sister Consolatio held Thresl's nose and mouth shut and in this way the afterbirth was brought forth.

Margaret washed the little girl and wrapped her in clean linen. I went upstairs. It was almost eleven in the morning.

I found my husband in his study room where he was having a bottle and some light breakfast with Pater Anselmus. He was very pleased when I told him that Thresl had a little daughter. "This is better than Last Rites," he said to the Pater and added that in a few days we would have a christening. Both wanted to go down at once and look at the child, but I said to wait some, as the chamber first had to be cleaned of all the blood and aired, for it was very smoky and stuffy in there.

When I came back Thresl was still in a faint while around her they were busy washing and scrubbing; she was being bandaged because she was still bleeding. Schabeyssen wanted to cauterize the cut, but I said I had enough of his works and that God surely would help Thresl to get well without any further cutting or burning.

Schabeyssen went over to Thresl and took the snakeskin off her neck. Then he made out his bill. It came to 25 florins. I found it rather dear, thinking that without Sister Consolatio's help he would not have been worth much to Thresl. I told him so, and he said if he could have the

child's Lucky Bonnet he would only ask for 15 florins. I said he should be ashamed of himself, that he had no right to ask for the Bonnet, that it was the child's, and paid him 15 florins and not a farthing more. The Hutterin wanted 10 florins (five for sleeping, perhaps), but without her the child might have died (which God prevented in His mercy), and so I did not begrudge her the money.

Sister Consolatio said that she would come by the next day to see how Thresl was faring. She joked and said I needn't worry—she would not sit on her again.

The next morning Thresl still was very weak and ran a high fever. Schabeyssen came again and brought a draught of caterpillars which he said was very good against childbed fever, but Thresl got agitated when he tried to make her drink it and knocked the glass out of his hand. The following day the fever subsided, with the help of God, so we did not need any caterpillars.

We give Thresl good strong soups, meat, eggs, honey, and wine. She has enough milk. This last Sunday we had little Brigitta baptized. She has blue eyes and very fine black hair. I would be curious to know whether the Count has dark hair, but I will not ask Thresl.

This was a long letter and I am now quite tired. My time is drawing near, and I hope and pray that God will make it easier for me than He has made it for my friend.

Thresl kisses your hands and will write to you as soon as she gains a little strength.

May God keep you in good health, Dear Mother.

Your obedient and loving daughter,
Barbara

Pray do not worry yourself about the Colloredo place. Yesterday we received a summons for Thresl from Steinschneyder, but Jacob took care of the Bailiff in no time. Steinschneyder will not be bothering Thresl for the next hundred years, I trust.

⋅◂❦▸⋅

BRIGITTA WIDOW CAMMERLOHER, IN SALZBURG, TO HER DAUGHTER, BARBARA SCHRETTER, IN VIENNA, WITH A LITTLE SILVER SPOON

This December 10, A.D. 1683

Dear Daughter:

I received your letter with the good news of Thresl's coming down with a little girl. Thank her in my name for christening the child after me. I am sending her this little spoon, which has been in my family for more than a hundred years, with my blessing.

I wish I could come down to be with you when your time comes (and it is near indeed), but my poor legs are plaguing me so much that I can hardly walk around in the house, let alone climb in a carriage. They are bleeding me a lot, but the veins still are thick and painful, albeit less at night when I have them propped up on two pillows.

Snow has been falling all through the night, but today we have sunshine, so Rosalia can hang up the wash in the garden.

Dear Daughter, I pray for you and that God may give a good, healthy child to you and to me a little grandson or granddaughter (for only men are partial to sons; a woman welcomes whatever the Lord sends her).

Your loving mother,
Brigitta Cammerloher, Widow

◄§§►

BARBARA SCHRETTER, IN VIENNA, TO HER MOTHER, BRIGITTA
WIDOW CAMMERLOHER, IN SALZBURG

This December 18, A.D. 1683

Dearest Mother:

Today we received your letter of December 10; the Taxis Mail is going a little slowly. I am quite worried about your health. Jacob says you should not allow too many of those quacks to treat you. If sleeping with your legs higher than your head gives you more relief from pain than all the bleeding and cauterizing, then by all means do not force yourself to let them bleed you. Rosalia is too old to take proper care of you. Pray be sure to have one of the Aichbichler girls come over for the heavy wash, and do not stand on your feet for hours on end.

Do not fret about me. I am feeling fine, thanks to the Good Lord. Margaret, the Hutterin, Thresl, and Cathrin will be with me, and I promise you that Schabeyssen will have to stay far away. And come spring, Jacob says, we all will travel to Salzburg to present you with your first grandchild (if God gives us one).

THERESIA KOHLRÖSER'S HAND

Dearest Mistress Cammerloher:

With all my heart I thank you for not having refused to be Godmother to my child and for letting it bear your name.

The little spoon is most precious to me. As I have no place to keep it, Barbara has put it in her jewel box for the time when my Brigitta will, with God's help, marry a good man, which will be more than her mother can say for herself.

Thank you also for having let my mother know that I am safe here, and that I do not have to fear the Bailiff anymore as long as I do not come back to Salzburg, for Vienna, after the Great Plague in '79, was declared "Asylum from the Secular Arm" for five years. (This Master Schretter has explained to me. He also explained it in a letter to the Bailiff, which letter might not have pleased the Bailiff any too well.)

Everybody here is good to me and I try to help Barbara as much as I can, which is not much right now for I am still somewhat weak, but I am getting stronger every day and therefore also will be of greater use to her.

Dearest Mistress Cammerloher, may the Lord keep you and give you back your health.

> I kiss your hands most gratefully.
> Thresl

Pray do not keep your legs too warm, as this makes the veins widen too quickly, which causes great pain, as I have seen my grandmother suffer.

My brother is still in Hungary, right now in the Pressburg garrison, and might come here on furlough any day, as a captain of the Caprara regiment, who had come by to visit Master Schretter, has told us. I am greatly frightened of what Poldl will say and do. Without Master Schretter here I would never dare face him.

❧

St. Stephen's Day, A.D. 1683

I intended to finish this letter almost a week ago and to have Cathrin run with it to the Taxis Mail. However, I did not get around to do it in time for I was called away from my task the other day: As I was settling down to write, in ran Cathrin, all excited. Count Starhemberg had sent a courier, asking when he could come to pay Jacob a sick call. Jacob, who is not so sick anymore, was greatly pleased and sent the courier back, saying that any day would be right. Therefore, the next afternoon the Count drew up at our house. Jacob and I received him at the foot of the staircase, and then the two men went into the library, where I served them sweets, Benedictine, and coffee that we had roasted from green beans (we got a few sacks from the Turkish camp).

The Count, a thin man with a neat wig and a very soft voice (I hardly could imagine him on the bastions), was most pleasant and said to me, "As long as we have men such as your husband, the Turks might as well look elsewhere for towns to take."

After the Count's departure it was already five o'clock and December 20 at that and no cleaning done for Christmas. I hired two girls from St. Anne's orphanage to do the scrubbing, but they were rather slow; therefore we could not begin to bake until the 23rd, and hardly finished in time.

On Christmas Eve, however, we had everything ready—candles, cakes, and presents. We had new skirts and shoes for Margaret and Cathrin, boots and doublets for Xaver and Vitus, and five florins over their regular wages for each. As for Thresl, I had saved some money and got her a new dress, a dark russet shade with some lace around the bodice. It suits her well indeed with her hair growing back. She was so pleased that she wept, for she had not worn a good new dress for many months, only twill skirts all patched up and wooden clogs and these last weeks some things of mine. Little Brigitta got a jacket and bonnet, and for Jacob (though he does not much care for fancy clothes) I had a ruffled shirt of very fine linen. Jacob gave me three golden combs all set with pearls for my hair. They are so beautiful that I hardly dare wear them for fear I might lose them.

We had a capon cooked and stuffed by Thresl (Jacob ate only from the white meat), and there was much laughter and good cheer at the dinner table. Afterward we went to Midnight Mass at St. Stephen's. It was very cold, but there was not much snow. We wondered first whether to take the carriage, but since there was no wind and I was wearing three skirts and a wrap around my coat, I felt no cold at all. So we walked to church, Jacob, Thresl, and I and also Vitus and Cathrin. Xaver stayed home and so did Margaret, who said she would rather mind little Brigitta than put her nose out in the cold.

There were many folk in church and it was lighted so

brightly by countless candles that one could see many of those saints and angels of stone one seldom can make out in the dark. Bishop Kollonitsch read the Three Masses. After Service Jacob went into the Sacristy and invited His Grace to a night cup, and the Bishop said, willingly, if we would drive to the house in his carriage, and this we did. I looked at Thresl and thought of the Colloredo bailiff and that he most surely would suffer a stroke if he could see her riding in the Bishop's coach.

At home we had spiced wine and Christmas cake and His Grace praised both very much. Jacob winked at me, for it was 'way after midnight, and His Grace had to say the Pontifical Mass the next day and certainly was not ready for communion. However, he is such a good man that the Lord, I trust, will forgive him.

This morning I am staying in bed a little longer. I breathe somewhat easier; Margaret says this means that the child has dropped and is making ready.

God willing you will have your first grandchild in a few days, and you will have a more cheerful time with it than you had with me—Father (God rest his soul) did make things hard for you, while I am fortunate indeed. Jacob is such pleasant company, I should do what I can to make him a good wife.

Thresl has just brought me my breakfast. It is ten o'clock, we have sunshine, and Jacob has gone to High Mass.

In a little while I will send for the Hutterin. Say a prayer, dear Mother, so that everything will go well.

I wish you God's Blessing for the New Year.

Your loving daughter,
Barbara

JACOB SCHRETTER, IN VIENNA, TO MONSIGNOR MICHAEL
KIRNSPERGER, DEACON OF ST. MARY'S AT INNSBRUCK

December 31, A.D. 1683

My Dear Friend,

God is inexorable.

Yesterday I lost Barbara, my dear wife, who died after giving birth to a son. The child lived for an hour.

Say a prayer for her soul and many for mine lest I quarrel with God's ways.

Your friend,
Jacob Schretter

THERESIA KOHLRÖSER, IN VIENNA, TO CAVALIERE ANDREA DE'
RICASOLI, PALAZZO RICASOLI RUCELLAI, FLORENCE, WITH A
LITTLE GOLD-AND-LEATHER–BOUND EDITION OF THE
DECAMERON

January 4, A.D. 1684

Your Grace:

My friend Barbara Schretter died last week after having been delivered of a son. The child died an hour later.

We had hoped to save her, but after the birth she was seized by a violent fever.

She called your name twice. As far as I could make out with the help of the little Italian I know, she fancied seeing you climbing up the Castle Tower. She stared at the ceiling and kept begging you to straighten the moonclock. After a while she quieted down, which was lucky, for we could no longer keep her husband from entering the sickroom. He came in and she must have recognized him, for she said in German, "It takes some reckoning. So much reckoning." Those were the last words she spoke.

We sent for Pater Anselmus. When he came, she was already sinking and knew no one. She was given Absolution and died shortly afterward.

I am sending you the little book Barbara has been keeping in her jewelry box. It should not be found among her things.

Your Grace's servant,
Theresia Kohlröser

The Hutterin (the midwife) told Margaret and me not to fret, that she was used to keeping her mouth shut, hearing every day far worse things from women afflicted with childbed fever.

CHURCH OF SANTA CROCE, FLORENCE
CAPPELLA DE' PAZZI

January 24, A.D. 1684

On behalf of Cavaliere Andrea de' Ricasoli:
Private Requiem Mass for Signora Barbara Schretter,
passed away in the Lord at Vienna on December 30, A.D.
1683. Mass by the Late Signor Frescobaldi at the request
of Cavaliere de' Ricasoli.

Present:
Cavaliere Andrea de' Ricasoli Rucellai
Cavaliere Orazio de' Ricasoli Rucellai
Count Lorenzo Magalotti

EPITAPH, CHURCHYARD OF THE MINORITES,
TOWN OF VIENNA

Hier liege ich mit dir, mein Leben
Deinetwegen beigesetzt.
Gott hat uns ein anders geben
Das uns für und für ergetzt.

Here I lie with thee, my Son,
God is now our Warden.
He has call'd and we have gone
To His Heavenly Garden.

JACOB SCHRETTER, IN VIENNA, TO MONSIGNOR MICHAEL
KIRNSPERGER, DEACON AT ST. MARY'S IN INNSBRUCK

This March 25, A.D. 1684

My Dear Friend:
Last night Vitus came back with the carriage. He tells me
that you had a comfortable journey and that you have
reached home in safety.

In wind and snow, over icy roads and none too healthy
yourself, you have come to my aid in my deepest sorrow
and have helped me to accept God's will. He has denied me
a life with Barbara, yet He granted me a year of hope and
joy. I will treasure it as long as I live.

These remaining years of mine which, in my blind grief, I
believed to prove barren and cold, will have a consolation: I
have adopted Thresl's child.

It is almost three months today that my wife and child are gone. It was a cold winter's day when we buried them; their coffin was covered with snow.

This morning, at the Minorites' churchyard, I saw the trees sprouting their first buds. A thrush sang in the grass. My heart, bitter or desperate no more, grew still. I sat down by the grave. At Angelus the stone cutter came and worked on the epitaph you had penned for me, your words of comfort in my darkest hour.

God bless you.

Your friend,
Jacob Schretter

As soon as my duties allow it (they are manifold, the new Mayor having delegated some of his endeavors to me), I shall come to Innsbruck for a few days.

Glossary

Absit laesio Maiestatis Let there be no offense against the Emperor's Majesty.

Absit omen May this not be a bad sign — deflecting formula after having spoken of possibly unlucky things. Comparable to more modern "God forbid."

Acherontic Scooped out of the bitter Acheron, one of the four rivers of the Greek Underworld. (The others are called Styx, Cocytus, and Lethe.)

Acta loquuntur Deeds speak (for me).

Amice dilectissime Most beloved Friend.

Black Manikins Twenty-eight cast-iron statues of princes and queens which as "mourners" surround the sarcophagus of Emperor Maximilian I (1478–1519) in the Court Chapel at Innsbruck. The statues were cast during the first half of the sixteenth century.

Boccaccio, Giovanni (1313–1375) Italian poet, author of the *Decameron*, a collection of one hundred stories told within ten days by seven ladies and three gentlemen who had fled the Great Plague in Florence and found themselves together in a country house not far from the city. The stories talk mostly about love, licit and illicit, of adventures, and sometimes of rather hair-raising jokes. The good are not always rewarded, the bad not always chastised. Husbands in particular get the short end of the stick.

149

Carolus Quintus (1500–1558)   Emperor Charles V. He renounced the Crown in 1556 and retired to the Monastery of San Yuste in Spain for the last two years of his life. To this day, in Austria he is considered the epitome of the gallant, courtly ruler.

In 1545 he had an affair with Barbara Blomberg, an innkeeper's daughter in Regensburg. Her son, Don Juan de Austria, became a naval hero who beat the Turks in the sea battle of Lepanto in the Adriatic in 1572.

Cataplasm   Application of thick, humid matter such as flour paste or mustard, covered by a piece of hot, damp linen. Was supposed to encourage sweating and the healing of wounds.

Cimento   Experiment (Italian). The *Accademia del Cimento*— Academy of Trial (and Error)—was founded in Florence in 1659. Its emblem was a burning furnace with three crucibles sitting on it and the motto *Provando e Riprovando*—"checking and checking again."

Coat Bag   In German, *Mantelsack*. A kind of bag made by using a big coat, which was put behind the saddle while its owner was riding. The ancestor of our duffel bag.

Copulant·   The priest who performs the ritual in a Catholic wedding.

Corruptio viscerum   Spoilage, breakdown of the intestines.

Cosimo—Cosimo de' Medici (1642–1723)   Grand Duke of Tuscany.

Courante   "The running one"—a lively dance in 3/4 time. Went out of fashion after 1700.

Date et dabitur vobis   Give and it will be given to you.

De profundis clamavi   "I cried out from the Depths"—from the Service for the Dead.

Dioneo   One of the three young men in Boccaccio's *Decameron*. Together with his two companions he fled from a public disaster, blissfully making love in the Tuscan hills.

Divine Poet — Dante Alighieri (1269–1321)   There is hardly a human situation in which an Italian, educated or not, could not come up with a quotation from Dante's *Divine Comedy*, preferably from the *Inferno*. The two other parts, *Purgatory* and *Paradise*, are less well known; damnation seems to be more fascinating than salvation.

Donatello — Donato di Niccolo di Betto Bardi (1386–1466)   Florentine sculptor, the pride of his fellow citizens. It was said that his works were not "statues" — they looked as if they could walk off their pedestals at any moment.

Dulce et decorum est pro patria mori, sed pro patria cacare?   It is sweet and glorious to die for one's homeland, but to shit for it?

Eritis sicut Deus   Ye shall be like God.

Est in votis   It is in the prayers; the outcome is pending.

Et haec meminisse iuvabit   Even this (hardship) will be a pleasure to remember.

Fama sufficiente   Of sufficiently bad reputation.

Figured Bass   An abbreviated way of writing down the accompanying bass voice for the keyboard by notes and chord numbers, a kind of musical shorthand. In the seventeenth century any player worth his salt was expected to be able to improvise over the bass line, yet to stick to the correct chord progressions.

Folía   Spanish dance, widely known at the time.

Fontange   Headdress, launched by Mlle. de Fontanges, one of Louis XIV's numerous mistresses. From a simple ribbon it proliferated into a structure of lace and wire. Was the fashion between 1680 and 1700.

Frescobaldi, Girolamo (1583–1643)   Italian composer and organist, greatly admired by Bach.

Fugit irreparabile tempus   The irretrievable time is fleeing.

Gracián, Baltasar (1601–1658)   Spanish writer and philosopher. He was taken by the idea of the heroic individual who gets the better of hostile surroundings. His stern, pessimistic maxims were widely read, especially in Italy, but seldom applied.

Guevara, Luis Velez de (1579–1644) Spanish poet and playwright. In addition to countless dramas he wrote a novel called *El Diablo Cojuelo* (The Limping Devil) in which Asmodeus, an indiscreet demon, shows the hero what is going on in the houses of a town by lifting off the roofs like so many box covers.

Hora certa, incerta die The hour is certain, the day uncertain.

Horror sempiternus Eternal fearsomeness. In the seventeenth century, the mountains were dreaded. Nobody would ever hike in them for pleasure; it was bad enough that one had to cross them to go to Italy or from there to Germany or France.

Huius Of this (month).

In illa die On *that* day (doomsday).

Iuris utriusque doctor (Doctor u.i.) Doctor of Both Laws— Canon and Secular.

Janissars Turkish elite troops, also the Sultan's bodyguards.

Kehraus "Sweep-out"—lively, concluding dance at weddings and other festivities.

Kollonitsch, Leopold Count of (1631–1707) Bishop of Neustadt. Vienna's heart and soul during the Turkish Siege. In 1686 he received his well-deserved cardinal's hat.

Lagrime di San Lorenzo "St. Lawrence's Tears"—popular name for the swarm of meteorites visible every year around August 11th, Feast of St. Lawrence.

Lente autem sicure Slowly but surely.

Lentil dish Figuratively: A disadvantageous bargain for the sake of instant gratification. This is an allusion to an episode from the Old Testament. Isaac, son of Abraham, had two sons, Esau and Jacob. One day Esau went hunting and came home, tired and hungry, to find Jacob busily preparing a dish of lentils. Esau asked for a portion, but Jacob refused to serve him until Esau gave him in exchange his birthright, that of the first-born.

Leopold I (1640–1705)   Ruler of the Holy Roman Empire. Was lucky to have had exceedingly able generals who saved him from several unpleasant situations. Is still called *Türkenpoldl* — "Turkish Poldi" — although he never saw action. Wrote delightful music.

Lucky Bonnet   Part of the amniotic bag which sometimes still covers the head of a newborn child. Such a "caul" was considered a talisman of good luck and would be carefully preserved. Was also widely used in medical concoctions.

Magalotti, Count Lorenzo (1637–1712)   Writer, scientist, traveler, diplomat, and perfume expert. Wrote an enormous amount of letters to his clever friends. Much of his correspondence — a gold mine for scholars — remains as yet unedited.

Manu propria   By his own hand. Formula at the end of documents. Used here as a parody of the official, bureaucratic style.

Mirabile dictu.   Amazing to say.

Montaigne, Michel Seigneur d'Eyquem (1553–1592)   French philosopher and writer. In his marvelous essays he sees his fellow humans as they are, warts and all, yet he never denies them his serene affection. He abhorred violence, was peacefully conservative, and managed to stay alive during the bloodiest religious wars France had ever seen.

Montecucculi, Count Raimondo (1609–1680)   Imperial general during the Thirty Years War. Wrote many treatises about military matters. Is sometimes lovingly quoted by economically unconcerned warriors: "To make war, one needs three things: Money, money, and money."

Morning star   A spiked, iron ball at the end of a stick or a rope.

Mustafa, Kara (1634–1683)   Grand Vizier of the Ottoman Empire. Stubborn, never knew when to retreat. After the failure before Vienna the Sultan sent him the Silken Cord, a tactful invitation which Mustafa chose to ignore. He was strangled on his way back to Constantinople.

Nata   Born. As used here, it means "maiden name."

Nunc dimittis   From *Nunc dimittis servum tuum* — (Now thou releasest thy servant) — part of the Prayer for the Dying during Absolution.

Optimus Artifex   The best of all artisans — God.

Paracelsus — Theophrastus Bombastus von Hohenheim (1493–1541)   Physician. Emphasized the healing power of plants and minerals. He despised the traditional teaching of the universities, and his lack of a degree and partial ignorance made him something of a butt for the medical establishment of his day. Yet with all his surprising intuition, his knowledge was haphazard, his reasoning arbitrary.

Pascal, Blaise (1623–1662)   French mathematician, physicist, and philosopher. His thinking "puts science in its place" and demands that the human soul, in the face of scientific and especially astronomic discoveries, be frightened at seeing Man so utterly lost in the Universe.

Passauerhof   The home and headquarters of the merchants from Passau, who had a branch in Vienna. During the Siege their building was used as a makeshift hospital.

Pater quem nuptiae demonstrant   A woman's lawful husband is to be considered the father of her child (Roman Law).

Pontus   From *Pontus Euxinus* — the Black Sea. As used here, exile among the country yokels. Allusion to Ovid, the Roman poet who was banished from the Capital for (allegedly) having had an affair with the Emperor's daughter. He was sent to Tomi, a desolate provincial town in what is today known as Rumania. Ovid pined away there, hoping to his last day to be reprieved. He never saw Rome again.

Probatum est   It has been proven, tried out. Sort of warranty seal for medical prescriptions.

Quodlibeticus   "Whatever is pleasing." As used here, a mixed bag of recipes, dream interpretations, prescriptions, household hints, etc.

Recitative   The prose sung between arias, duets, etc., in an opera or oratorio. It serves to further the action.

Rector Magnificus   The Magnificent Ruler—highest magistrate of a university.

Red Flux   Bloody dysentery, a highly contagious intestinal infection. Occurs often during wars, sieges, earthquakes—whenever even elementary sanitary rules cannot be followed.

Redi, Francesco (1626–1698)   Italian physician, writer, and poet. His preoccupation with worms paid off: He discovered the *Redia*, a stick-shaped larva which constitutes the second development stage of the liver maggot, a dangerous livestock parasite that can now be destroyed by chemotherapy.

Refutatio per scientiam   Refutation through scientific arguments.

Ricasoli   Noble Florentine family, already prominent in the fifteenth century. They counted warriors among their men as well as poets, writers, and scientists. In the nineteenth century there lived Bettino Ricasoli, called the Iron Baron, patriot, politician, fighter for Italy's unification and successful wine grower, as you can read on many a straw-clad Chianti bottle: "Filled on the premises—Brolio, Ricasoli, Italia."

Salva Venia   Literally, "With your favor intact." Whenever one had to talk of something vulgar or revolting in the presence of a person of standing, the phrase served as a defusing device, meaning: "I have to use this expression for the sake of clarity—there is no disrespect meant."

Salve atque vale   Hail and farewell.

Sapienti sat   A word to the wise is sufficient.

Saraband   Spanish dance, slow and stately, in 3/4 time.

Senna juice (Folia sennae)   A violent laxative, often taken in the belief that it would cause a woman to abort.

Si cum Jesuitis   From *Si cum Jesuitis, non cum Jesu itis* — wordplay: "If you go with the Jesuits, you do not go with Jesus."

S.J.   Abbreviation of *Societatis Jesu*, Society of Jesus, pertaining to the Jesuits.

Slipper   The Iron Slipper — a torture instrument shaped like a shoe. With the aid of a crank it could be tightened until the foot was crushed.

Soldatesca   All the soldiers — a group term similar to "the citizenry."

Sugar Hat   At the time, crystal sugar was sold in two-foot-high cones similar to a dunce's cap.

Swedish Drink   Torture method, perfected by the Swedish troops during the Thirty Years War. Slop from the pigsty or the cesspool would be heated and poured down the victim's throat.

Taxis Mail   Named after Franz von Taxis (1459–1517), who set up a regular mail service under Emperor Maximilian I. The Taxis family had a monopoly on the office of the Postmaster General in the Holy Roman Empire.

Theophrastian   According to the principles of Theophrastus B. Paracelsus.

Thesaurus vanus est filia patri suo   A daughter is a useless treasure to her father.

Three Places   Heaven, Hell, and Purgatory.

Tiziano — Titian (1477–1576)   Full name — Tiziano Vecellio. Italian painter, one of the greatest. His goddesses, courtesans, and Madonnas often have reddish-gold hair. Emperor Charles V, of whom he painted a wonderful portrait (Pinakothek, Munich), had a profound admiration for him. Titian died in his ninety-ninth year, and legend has it that he was in such good condition to the very end that it took the plague to fell him.

Viragines   From Virago—mannish, ungraceful female.

Virtus laudata crescit   Virtue, commended, increases.

Wallenstein, Albrecht Prince of, Duke of Friedland (1583– 1634)   Imperial Generalissimo in the Thirty Years War. He was a military genius, but grew too big for his boots, as well as for the comfort of Emperor Ferdinand. Because of secret negotiations with the Swedes he was accused of high treason, demoted, and then dispatched by a hired killer, Captain Deveroux from Ireland.

Wirtschaft   Literally: hostelry or inn. Here, a special kind of dance party during Carnival, much favored by the Austrian aristocracy of the seventeenth century. A castle or palace was transformed into a tavern for one night, host and hostess played the innkeeper and his wife. The guests would arrive disguised as coachmen, stable boys, soldiers, milkmaids, cooks, etc. Young noblemen liked to invite girls from burghers' families to a Wirtschaft, sometimes to the latters' regret.

Bibliography

Colerus, Johann. *Oeconomia Ruralis et Domestica.* Mainz: J. B. Schönwetter's Widow, 1672.

Magalotti, Lorenzo. *Lettere del Conte Lorenzo Magalotti.* Firenze: G. Manni, 1736.

Magalotti, Lorenzo. *Lettere scientifiche ed erudite del Conte Lorenzo Magalotti.* Firenze: Per i Tartini e Franchi, 1721.

Hocke, Nicolaus. *Kurtze Beschreibung dessen was in wehrender türckischer Belägerung der statt Wienn von 7. Julij bis 12. Septembris 1683 passiret.* Wien: L. Voigt, 1685.

Anguisciola, Leandro. *Assedio di Vienna d'Austria intrapreso li 14 luglio 1683 dagli Ottomani etc. Racconto istorico di L.A. Con due piante in rame delineate dal Sig. Leandro Anguisciola.* Modona: Stamperia di D. Degni, 1684.

Thun, Franz Graf von. *A memorial which his excellency the count of Thunn, envoy extraordinary from His Imperial Majesty, presented to the King of Brittain the 3/13 of October, touching the raising of the siege from before Vienna.* London: printed for L. Curtis, 1683.

Redi, Francesco. *Lettere di Francesco Redi,* 2d ed. fiorentina. Firenze: G. Cambiagi, stampator granducale, 1779–95.

Vienna Town Archives. *Town accounts, testaments and deeds 1660–1690.*

Frescobaldi, Girolamo. *Primo Libro d'Arie musicali per cantarsi nel Gravicembalo e Tiorba* etc. Firenze: Gio. Batista Landini, 1630.